COLTER SONS BOOK 4

THE RESOURCEFUL
STOCKMAN

Karen Baney

desert life
media

The Resourceful Stockman: Colter Sons Book 4
By Karen Baney

Publisher:
Desert Life Media, LLC
Gilbert, AZ 85295

www.karenbaney.com

Printed in the United States of America

ISBN-979-8-9863369-3-0

For the word of the Lord is upright,
and all his work is done in faithfulness.
He loves righteousness and justice;
the earth is full of the steadfast love of
the Lord.

—Psalm 33:4-5

———

Behold, the eye of the Lord is on those
who fear him, on those who hope in his
steadfast love, that he may deliver their
soul from death and keep them alive in
famine. Our soul waits for the Lord;
he is our help and our shield.
For our heart is glad in him,
because we trust in his holy name.

—Psalm 33:18-21

CHAPTER 1

DEACON

I'm Deacon Colter, number four out of five Colter sons. In some ways, I'm the spitting image of my papa. I have his same brown hair and his same brown eyes. Same build. It's like looking into a mirror and seeing myself at sixty. He's still a pretty handsome fella, especially in Mama's eyes.

Around my twenty-fourth birthday, I accepted that I'm completely different from my brothers. James is a successful entrepreneur at the railroad. Sam is smart and finally, after six years, has become a skilled rancher, more so than I ever expected. Boone is still wild and crazy, even after the birth of his son. Preston, well, he's the drifter of the family, and no one knows what he's up to.

Me? I am the most resourceful of us brothers. My gut instincts have never failed me. When I look at something, I immediately see the details and parts. Like my sister-in-law's typewriter. When I look at it, I see things that others don't. A tweak here or there would make it considerably more efficient.

With such skills, it might seem odd that I became a veterinarian. Yet, there are a lot of similarities between figuring out how an animal works versus figuring out how machinery works. There are certain rules and laws of God's nature that apply to animals. Others miss subtle signs that are clues to the animal's health, but I see them clearly.

After apprenticing under my mentor, Ray Sawyer, for several years, I became the staff veterinarian for the Prescott Stockyards. I preferred working directly with the animals and limiting my interaction with people. Animals don't get upset when I needed to stack hay bales perfectly symmetrical. Never offended a cow if I told it one of its eyes was slightly bigger than the other.

Because I notice things that others don't, I often find myself in awkward situations with people. Things that are out of place compel me to organize them logically. If a woman has a freckle an inch below the corner of her left eye, or if one side of her mouth tilts down more than the other, I notice it. Unfortunately, that trait rubs most people the wrong way.

The only person who knows the full extent of my secret is my best friend, Grady Thatcher. When his parents were murd-ered six years ago, he came to live with us at Colter Ranch because his older sister, Ellie Mae, married Sam. We became instant friends. As my roommate under my parents' roof, he quickly noticed my odd behavior. I hid it well from my family, but I never could hide it from Grady. The thing was, it didn't bother him. He accepted me as I am. He even helped me try to control it.

Since no woman would ever want a man as odd as me, I resolved myself to the life of a bachelor. At least that was my plan until I met the perfectly organized and resplendent Lilian Harper.

———

GRADY

And my name is Grady Thatcher. Like Deacon said, I am not one of the Colter sons. From the day I moved to Colter Ranch, they made me feel like part of the family.

Like Deacon, I am a veterinarian, also mentored by Ray Sawyer after Deacon took the job at the stockyards. My love for animals started on my family's farm outside of Chino Valley. I grew up around horses, a milk cow, barn cats, and even a dog when I was a little boy.

Even though I learned to laugh again at the ranch, my family's farm and my parents' murder were never far from my mind. After six long years, there was still no justice for their deaths. I witnessed the whole thing. The man who shot my mama—it seared his face into my memory. I didn't let it get me down most days. Still, that man must pay for what he did.

Little did I know, one day I'd meet him face to face, and I'd have to make the toughest decision of my life. Nothing could have prepared me for that.

CHAPTER 2

Prescott, Arizona Territory
January 23, 1893

DEACON

My day started like most Mondays. Grady and I joined my family for breakfast at my brother's house promptly at seven o'clock. Then we saddled our horses and rode to town. While Grady rode on to the veterinary clinic, I veered toward the stockyards on Sergeant, my blood bay gelding.

When I arrived at the stockyards, I stabled Sergeant before I entered my office. I flipped through the paperwork for the newly arrived cattle. One group of thirty head needed inspection.

I donned my lab coat and grabbed my bag. Then I entered the corral, where we isolated new cattle from the other livestock. Because they were Polled Shorthorns, I carefully checked them for any signs of fever ticks.

After an hour, I examined the paperwork more closely. I compared the brands and bill of sales with the brands on the cattle. The paperwork claimed the brand was an I Bar 8. I wasn't familiar with that brand, so I scrutinized it.

Something looked unusual with the eight. It wasn't a normal eight that narrows in the center. Instead, the right side appeared smooth, like a nine. And the "I" looked like they branded it over a "T".

Brand burners.

My stomach tightened. The more I studied the brands, the more I knew the original brand was T Bar 9, a brand that belonged to Jack Thompson. Each animal had slight variations of the smoothness on the right side of the eight. Sometimes, the bottom line of the "I" was not perfectly perpendicular to the center line of the "I".

I sighed as I headed back to my office to read through the paperwork in more detail. The bill of sale claimed the owner purchased the cattle from a B. Irving. Even though the address was in Yavapai County, I didn't recognize the name. The initials on the paperwork showed that my coworker, Bart Mason, received the cattle at the stockyard.

Once I set the paperwork aside, I returned to finish the health examination of the cattle. A few hours made no difference in determining who burned the brand.

By two o'clock, I wrapped up my assessment. The cattle were healthy and free from ticks and disease. I signed the appropriate section of the paperwork. Then I took the paperwork to my boss, Derek Gardner.

To prepare myself for the clutter and chaos of his office, I took a deep breath. Disorganization and disorder bothered me. Even though it was not normal to be disturbed by such a scene, the anxiety built inside me, anyway. As I rolled my shoulders in circles, I knocked twice on his door.

"Deacon," he greeted me as I stepped into his office.

My eyes quickly cataloged the chaos, which made my skin crawl. I shook off the thoughts and handed him the paperwork while I shared my suspicions about the brand.

"It looks like Jack Thompson's brand underneath and that someone burned over it."

"Let's look."

As he stepped into the hallway, I was relieved to leave his office.

Before I finished showing him the brands, my mentor, Ray Sawyer, entered the corral along with Grady. I brought them up to speed on my discovery.

Grady crouched down to eye level with the brand. He ran his fingers over the smooth side of the eight.

"Feels like more hair overgrowth by the smooth side," he said.

"Yup," I said.

"Same with the upper line of the 'I'."

"I thought the same."

"Think you are spot on," Grady confirmed.

Ray took a quick look and agreed. Though I appreciated their support, Derek believed me without hearing their thoughts.

"Can you report this to the livestock inspection office?" Derek asked.

"Sure thing."

As I walked back to my office, Ray and Grady followed me. I set my bag in its proper place as I hung my lab coat on the hook on the back of the door. Then I grabbed my jacket and the paperwork before I turned my attention to my guests.

"What brings you by?" I asked.

"Let's talk while we walk," Ray suggested.

I held the door open for them and we headed toward the livestock inspection office.

"Ray is leaving Prescott," Grady said. "He has a proposal

for us we should consider."

"It's been my pleasure to have mentored both of you over the years. Deacon, you have a keen eye for anything suspicious, like with that brand. That was one of the best brand forgeries I've seen yet, but you figured it out immediately."

"Thank you."

"And Grady, your skill at detecting early signs of illness, especially in livestock, is superb."

I stopped for a moment to study Ray. Usually, the compliments flowed right before he asked us to do something unpleasant, like mucking stalls.

Ray laughed. "Don't worry, what I'm about to suggest is something good, a unique opportunity I believe you are both perfectly suited for."

"Go on," I said, still wary of his motives.

"I have been appointed the Veterinarian General of the Territory to oversee more changes in the Sanitary and Livestock Commission. Since we are on our way to the livestock inspection office, I know you are already familiar with the work done on behalf of the committee."

I gave him a sharp nod, hoping he'd get to the point soon.

"Well, we are hiring several new full-time livestock inspectors. We need two more here in Yavapai County."

"And?"

Grady sighed dramatically. "And he wants us to apply for those openings!"

My chest tightened and I clenched my jaw. Patterns and routines comforted and calmed me. I arrived at the office at five 'til eight every morning. I took lunch at precisely noon. Ellie Mae served supper at six. I wore a blue or a white button-down shirt every day with my denim pants. I thrived in a predictable life. That's why I lived at the ranch instead of in town. The ranch was familiar and scheduled. The same day after day, year after year.

"It will be great, Deacon. We will travel all over the county. We'll meet new people and we'll be active participants in stopping livestock theft."

Grady's list of positives caused my throat to constrict even though I understood his motivation. He wanted to help stop rustlers. Rustlers like the ones that murdered his parents.

The muscles in my shoulders tensed. "I don't know."

Ray said, "Just go talk to Perry Quinn. He's the new Supervisor of Livestock Inspection. Listen to his vision. If you don't like it, then don't take the job."

"Please, Deacon, you know what this would mean to me," Grady implored.

I did. I also knew no one else would watch his back like me. As my mouth went dry, I resolved to battle the demons inside of me in order to support my best friend. He needed that job as much as I needed uniformity.

"Alright. I suppose we can talk to him while I'm there to report the brand violation."

Grady grinned from ear to ear.

———

GRADY

I expected to go through a much longer list of arguments to convince Deacon to apply for the job. It surprised me when he capitulated so quickly. Certainly, he understood the job would be completely unpredictable and devoid of structure. Unlike most people, Deacon required pre-dictability and structure. Without it, he'd struggle inside, where no one could see. I felt humbled that he would sacri-fice for a friend, for me.

As we entered the livestock inspection office, Ray said his farewells to us.

The building was not very large. An open lobby area held four chairs along one wall. Above the chairs was a map of the entire county. On the opposite wall hung drawings of registered brands for cattle, horses, and sheep. Across from the entrance behind a desk, a painting hung on the wall. There were several bookshelves near the desk.

When Deacon set his paperwork on the top of a short bookshelf, I held back a groan. He started removing the sketches of the brands from the wall. It was futile to hope he would leave the brands in the order they hung.

"Deacon, please stop. They may have a reason they hung the brands that way."

"It makes no sense. A person could not memorize them or spot the subtle differences. There's a better way."

The door to an adjoining office opened and a young woman with strawberry blond hair and light blue eyes walked toward the desk. She stopped short when she saw Deacon. As a frown creased her forehead, I wanted to melt into the floorboards.

"What do you think you are doing?" she asked as she propped her hands on her hips.

"I'm fixing this."

My jaw tightened. Sometimes Deacon was his own worst enemy. She would have received any other word be-sides "fix" better.

"There is nothing to fix, Mister. I organized them by the date registered."

"I know."

Fire burned in her eyes, spurring me to do something before I lost the best opportunity to find my parents' killers.

CHAPTER 3

LILIAN

As I stepped out of Perry Quinn's office, a tall young man with a dark brown cowboy hat stood in front of my wall of brands, which no longer hung on the wall in the registered date order. Instead, he spread the papers out on the floor.

My ire rose, as did my voice. The room felt warmer than a few minutes ago. "What do you think you're doing?"

"Fixing it."

Of all the...

"Miss?" a lanky young man with a black cowboy hat and tan duster stepped between me and the usurper.

"My name is Grady Thatcher. That's Deacon Colter, the vet for the stockyards. He's here to report a theft." He waved some papers in front of me.

As I snatched the paperwork from Grady's hand, I glared at Deacon. Then my eyes dropped to the paperwork. I skimmed through the key points.

"We're also here to speak to Mr. Quinn about the open positions."

I jerked my head toward Deacon. "He's got a funny way

of making a good first impression."

"Miss, what is your name?"

"Lilian. Lilian Harper." I glowered at Deacon in his crisp white shirt, denim pants, and tan leather jacket.

"Miss Harper, my apologies for my friend's behavior. He has a special talent for seeing things in a way no one else does. From my experience, he means no harm and most of the time his ideas work out alright."

Perry stood leaning in the doorway of his office. He crossed his arms over his chest and studied both Deacon and Grady, yet he said nothing. I frowned when I noticed the edge of his mouth curl up.

"Anyway, Miss Harper, if you dislike what he does, I'll help you put them back in the registered date order."

Even though the fire in me diminished because of Grady's soft demeanor, I remained standing. I shoved the paperwork at Grady.

When my lips parted, Perry held up a hand to stop me. He said quietly, "Let's see how this works out."

I nodded as the pattern Deacon created became clear. He grouped all the brands that started with an "A" together. Then, similar variations were next to each other. All the lazy "A's" followed the flying "A's" and so on. If two brands included the same letter and symbol, such as "C bar", he placed those brands next to each other. He mixed the brands regardless of the type of livestock. I was glad I coded them with a "C" for cattle, "H" for horse, "S" for sheep, and "O" for other before I originally hung them. Otherwise, I was not certain I could group them by animal later.

As he finished tacking up the last one, he turned to face me. He crossed his arms over his broad chest. Then his dark brown eyes locked with mine.

"Ask me to name any brand for any letter," he said.

"T."

He turned his back to the wall, and I suddenly felt warm. My, he was a handsome man with his angled jaw and intense eyes.

"T Bar 9. T Bar A. Rocking T C."

My eyes widened. "How did you…"

"This way here lets you see like brands together. The subtle variations make it easier to memorize quickly. I'll bet Grady could name off all the 'B's' without looking."

Grady obliged his friend and turned his back to the wall. Then he recited the brands with a "B" flawlessly. "That last one is for sheep only."

"Show off," Deacon muttered under his breath. The hint of a smile tugged on his lips.

Perry cleared his throat before I could respond. "I like it." He motioned the men in his direction.

As Deacon walked past my desk, he suggested, "A picture of a cow, horse, and sheep on each one would help."

I narrowed my eyes at his retreating back while Perry led them into his office.

As I sat at my desk, I shifted my position, still unsettled by the handsome stranger who had reorganized my wall. I was Perry's secretary. It was my job to do that. And I needed that job. It provided for my sisters and me.

Moving to Prescott rescued us from the unpredictability and danger of life with my father. Even with my older brother, Shane, running the ranch, the family never knew when Papa would sell half the stock and gamble it away on some new scheme. Or hide sinister men at the ranch. We wearied living day to day, not knowing if we would have money for food or if we'd face harm.

So, at twenty-three, I figured I ought to strike out on my own. I sent for my nineteen-year-old sister, Justine, and my seventeen-year-old sister, Hayley, after I landed a job, which provided enough money for the basics. They were still looking for employment, so I needed to keep my job. Hopefully, Deacon's stunt didn't jeopardize my standing with Perry.

After an hour, Perry opened the door and shook Grady's hand and then Deacon's.

"Welcome aboard," he said. "I look forward to you starting next Monday."

I swallowed down the bile as I imagined all the ways Deacon Colter would make my job more difficult.

"This is Miss Harper," Perry introduced me. "She runs the office and you will work closely with her for your assign-ments, especially if I am traveling."

"Please," I said as I stood. "Call me Lilian." I forced a less-than-sincere smile onto my face.

"Lilian," Deacon said my name softly.

My heart skipped a beat, and I scolded the deceitful organ for its reaction. He held out a hand for me to shake. Though I felt awkward, I shook it anyway. Tingles tickled trails up my arm at his soft touch.

"I want to apologize for… For taking over the branding wall without asking your permission. I did not mean to offend you."

He released his hold on my hand, but his dark brown eyes remained fixed on mine. I swallowed the lump in my throat as my breathing shallowed.

"I know I come across as impolite and pushy. I don't mean to."

He straightened first one stack of paperwork on my desk and then the next. My nostrils flared, and I bit the inside of my lip to keep from growling. I imagined smacking his hand away from my things.

"My mind just reorganizes things, and I feel compelled to listen to it," he said as he shifted the can of pencils on my desk by a fraction of an inch.

"I know it is… Off-putting. Forgive me for offending you."

As I moved the can of pencils back with a clunk, I took a deep breath. "Apology accepted."

My tone came out harsher than I intended, especially since I truly appreciated his apology.

"See you next week," he said as he touched his fingertips to the brim of his hat. Then he turned and left the building.

"Would you like me to stay and help you reorganize the brands?" Grady offered.

I shook my head. "Your friend would only put them back this way next week."

"I'm truly sorry about that."

I waved my hand in the air. "It's fine. I can see the rationale of his approach."

"Good day, Miss Harper," Grady said, as he offered a sympathetic smile. Then he left the building.

I sank into my chair and expelled a loud breath.

Perry chuckled.

"What's so funny?"

"Don't worry, Lilian, I won't be replacing you any time soon. I do like Deacon's approach, though. Be open to new ways of looking at things, especially any suggestions from the inspectors. The Sanitary and Livestock Commission is still relatively new. It's unconventional thinking that will pave the way for the future of how we inspect livestock and build a case against rustlers."

"I see how his way makes it easier to memorize the brands," I conceded.

"Good. If it makes you feel any better, he mentioned the

scars on my face."

My eyes widened. "You're not serious."

"Yes ma'am."

The man had no couth. I shook my head before I expelled another breath. "Since I'll be working with them, can you tell me about them?"

"Deacon Colter is from the Colter clan, one of the larger cattle ranches in the county. Larson Stables and Colter Ranch are just outside of town to the northeast. His father, Will Colter, is the earliest rancher in the area and a friend of mine."

"I see," I said, as my shoulders slumped. I better tread carefully with our new hires.

"Both Deacon and Grady live on the ranch. They share a house, as Grady said, 'for now.' Grady's sister is married to Deacon's older brother, Sam. Both Deacon and Grady are friends and vets, both mentored by Ray Sawyer."

Just last week, I read the memo announcing Ray's new position with the Territory. Sounded like he would move to Phoenix.

"They are both fine young men and will be great additions to our staff of inspectors. Though I may pair them together instead of sending them out independently. Seems like Grady is better with people."

I snorted. "I won't argue with that."

CHAPTER 4

DEACON

As I returned to the stockyards, I was not glad Perry Quinn hired us. Anxious? Yes. Terrified? Possibly. Happy? Not in the slightest. I hung my jacket on its hook. Then I took off my hat and ran a hand through my hair.

Of all the social faux pas I could have committed... Shaking my head, I imagined kicking myself. I can't believe I mentioned Perry's scars on his face. I knew they were from a fire a long time ago. And I knew it was socially unacceptable to say anything about them. Unfortunately, when I got nervous, I failed to maintain as much control as normal. When those words flew out of my mouth, I looked at Grady. I thought he might haul me outside and smack me up the side of my head. I would have deserved it.

Yet Perry hired us anyway.

I put my hat back on my head and glanced at the clock. A half hour until quitting time. I headed to Derek's office and gave him a quick update. Even though I gave him my notice, I told him I might help from time to time if I wasn't busy with livestock inspections. He eagerly accepted the arrangement.

I gathered my things from the office and headed out to the stables to saddle Sergeant. By the time I finished, Grady joined me.

"Deacon." He shook his head. "Sometimes I don't know what to do with you. You almost cost us that job today."

"I know. I'm sorry," I said as I frowned.

"It's a miracle Lilian even accepted your apology."

I sighed. Lilian. Beautiful seemed like an inadequate word to describe her. Stunning. Gorgeous. Resplendent. Her strawberry blond hair and soft blue eyes drew me in. She wasn't like those twiggy women in town who would be blown over by a stiff wind. No, she had some meat on her bones in all the right places.

Grady groaned as I mounted my horse. "You like her."

"No, I don't."

He laughed. "You do. Your face never lies to me."

I kicked Sergeant into motion toward home. Grady brought Sunbeam up next to us.

"I'm glad we got this job. Maybe I'll finally be able to track down the man who murdered my parents."

"I'm sorry if I put you through undue stress. I'll do everything I can to help you find the rustlers."

"I know you will. I appreciate you trying this new venture. It'll challenge you."

I snorted. Intimidate was more like it.

We arrived home at a quarter 'til six like normal, and we took care of our horses, washed up, and joined the family for supper at Sam's house. I really liked that Ellie Mae continued to invite us to eat with the family, despite her growing number of children. She even hosted my birthday party last weekend.

As Grady held the door open, the cries of Sam's children resounded in the room. My sister, Vi, tried to wrangle two-year-old Brody. Sam scolded four-year-old Sterling. Baby Ashley cried from her bassinet. I walked over and scooped up my niece into my arms.

"Shh," I murmured to her as I bounced her up and down in my arms. Grady handed me a bottle, and I held it for Ashley. My heart warmed as she ate greedily from it.

"Someday, Ash, maybe we'll give you a few cousins to play with," I whispered.

When she finished eating, I took a cloth and tossed it over my shoulder. Then I burped her.

Ellie Mae and Mama set supper on the table. Even though I should sit for the meal, I couldn't put the sweet, warm bundle down yet. Every time I held Ashley, the longing to marry and become a father grew stronger. I had no right to such dreams. No woman would ever accept my idiosyncrasies.

While Papa prayed over the meal, I held her. Then I gently lowered her into her bassinet before I took my usual seat at the table.

"We got a new job," Grady shared, as his eyes lit with excitement.

"I thought you enjoyed being a vet," Ellie Mae said.

"We do. But this is a special job that uses our veterinary skills and Deacon's observations and eye for detail."

"What job is that?" Vi asked.

"Livestock inspector," I answered without looking up, as I carefully cut my roast into equal-sized pieces. When I finished cutting the meat, I started eating.

"We start on Monday," Grady said, "and will work with Perry Quinn. We will travel all over the county inspecting livestock for disease and for brand violations."

I glanced up from my food and studied my parents. Mama quickly masked her concern, but not before I noticed.

"Traveling? Are you sure, Deacon?" Mama asked.

She knew me well, but I nodded anyway. If I spoke, my voice would betray my true feelings.

I breathed a sigh of relief when the conversation turned to other topics. As soon as supper was over, I excused myself and headed over to my house.

When I entered, I tossed my things on the table and headed to my room. I paced the length of the room several times, wondering what I had gotten myself into. I was foolish to think I could be a livestock inspector.

A knock sounded on the door.

"Deacon, do you want to talk?" Grady asked.

"No."

"Alright. I'll put your things where they belong."

I grunted. Then I sat on the edge of my bed. I needed to stop thinking about the traveling part of it. Somehow, I needed to make something feel routine and normal about my new job. And I had to figure it out soon.

Forty minutes later, I exited my bedroom and looked out the window that faced my parents' house. The light in the parlor shone, so I hurried across the yard and knocked twice on their door.

"Evening, Deacon," Mama greeted me as she pulled her shawl tighter around her shoulders. After she stepped aside to allow me to enter, she closed the door behind me.

"Where's Vi?"

"She saw you walking over, so she retired to her room to read."

I nodded before I straightened all the chairs at the table.

Mama handed me a coffee mug. I sat down and she sat across from me as Papa joined us.

"What's on your mind?" she asked softly.

Before I took a sip, I turned the mug around three times. Then I set it back down. My leg bobbed up and down underneath the table.

"That bad?" Papa asked.

I cleared my throat and my leg stopped moving, still clueless how to unpack all the thoughts running around in my head.

"This new job. I know it's important to Grady."

Mama smiled and reached out for my hand. She squeezed it. "Aren't you a little excited about it?"

I shook my head vehemently. Then I sipped my coffee for a bit.

"And there's Lilian."

Papa took a sip of his coffee as his eyes sparkled.

"Who's Lilian?" Mama asked.

"She's Perry Quinn's secretary at the livestock inspection office."

The corner of Mama's mouth twitched.

I sighed loudly. "She's real pretty. Grady thinks I like her. I guess I do. But I really…"

My leg bobbed up and down again. I took a deep breath and let it out in one big rush.

"I rearranged all the brands on the wall and offended her. I don't think she'll give me the time of day."

"Why do you say that?" Mama asked.

"What woman would? I'm terrible with people. Without trying, I offend pretty much everyone I meet. Mama, I told her I was fixing her work. I can't believe I said that."

I grabbed a handful of my hair and tugged.

"Did you apologize?" Papa asked.

"Of course. But not before the damage was done."

Slowly, Mama pushed away from the table and stood. She retrieved her Bible and brought it back to the table. I watched as she flipped toward the New Testament. Then she read, "Therefore I tell you, do not be anxious about your life, what you will eat or what you will drink, nor about your body, what you will put on. Is not life more than food, and the body more than clothing? Look at the birds of the air: they neither sow nor reap nor gather into barns, and yet your heavenly Father feeds them. Are you not of more value than they?"

Then her gaze connected with mine as she recited the rest of the verse from Matthew from memory. "And which of you by being anxious can add a single hour to his span of life?"

As my shoulders slumped forward, I looked down at the coffee in my mug.

"Deacon," Papa said. "Stop stealing time from your life by being anxious about a job you haven't started."

"And by fretting over one interaction with Lilian," Mama added. "You are a good man. You care deeply for others and are fiercely loyal. Certainly, you have a few odd tendencies. But I think once Lilian sees your heart, she will understand."

"Especially if God had a hand in you meeting her," Papa added.

I turned the mug around three times. Then I gulped the rest of the coffee before I set it down.

Mama reached for my hand again. She held it for a minute. I looked up and studied her brilliant blue eyes. "I know you have an excellent memory. Take that to heart: Which of you by being anxious can add a single hour to his span of life?"

"Yes, Mama."

She released my hand. "Would you like more coffee?"

"No thanks. I should head back home."

I stood and hugged Mama. Then Papa walked me to the door and squeezed my shoulder.

"When you're alone and thinking about your quirks, don't make them bigger than they are. Like your mother said, you are a good man. Any woman who gets to know you will be the better for it."

"Thanks, Papa."

"Good night, son."

As the air grew colder, I hurried across the yard back to my house. Grady had retired for the night, so I did, too. Maybe Lilian would warm up to me in time.

CHAPTER 5

GRADY

When I entered the house, Deacon's things lay scattered across the tabletop, and I feared the worst. He never just tossed his things anywhere. Everything had a place and everything went in its place, unless something troubled him deeply.

I checked on him, but he didn't want to talk, so I put his things away instead. Then I lit a fire in the fireplace and sat across from it in my favorite chair.

Lord, please help Deacon become comfortable with this new job. Help him find joy in it and not just suffer through it for me.

He was the most loyal man I'd ever met. Yet, I wanted the job to be something he learned to enjoy. As I headed to bed, I tried to let go of my worry.

Over the next week, time flew by. Ray and I worked with one other vet, Brad Blackburn, who would take over the clinic the following week.

Deacon seemed to settle down the closer our start date came. I, on the other hand, slept less and less. The nightmares about my parents' murder plagued me the entire weekend before our first day.

When I woke late on Monday, Deacon thrust a mug of coffee in my hand and gave me a wrapped biscuit stuffed with egg and bacon. Despite his rough exterior, I saw the concern in his eyes. Once we rode toward town, he finally spoke.

"You alright?"

After I shook my head, I bit into the biscuit. When I swallowed, I said, "I didn't sleep well. The images of my mama being shot… In the… Head."

I coughed.

"I know it's hard. We'll do our best to find the men who did it."

"Thanks, Deacon."

He smiled sympathetically.

By the time we reached the outskirts of town, I finished my breakfast. Once we arrived at the office, we hitched the horses to the post out front. Then we entered the building.

Lilian greeted me warmly and Deacon warily. I couldn't blame her. I just hoped she would soften toward him once she got to know him. The way he looked at her told me he fancied her more than he'd admit to himself, much less to me. I wanted my friend to find love and happiness. If Lilian was the woman he chose, I'd help.

"Morning, Miss Harper," Deacon said. "If you don't mind, I'd like to sketch a copy of the brands to take with us."

"Not at all. Please, call me Lilian." Her smile was genuine as she handed Deacon some paper and a pencil. I asked for the same.

While we worked, a thirty-something-year-old man enter-ed the office. He wore all black and a stoic expression that bordered on anger.

"Morning, Valentine," he said.

Lilian stiffened. "Morning. Please stop calling me that."

His face broke into a broad, toothy grin. Deacon straightened and turned toward the man.

"No need to get your petticoats ruffled, Valentine. Just came for my assignment from Quinn."

When Deacon took a step forward, I swallowed away the tightness in my throat.

"The lady asked you to stop calling her that."

For once, I was grateful for Deacon's gigantic size. He stood several inches taller than the man in black. His shoulders were significantly broader, too.

"I think you owe her an apology."

I pretended to sketch the brands.

"Who says?"

"Deacon," Lilian said as she placed a hand on his arm. "It's fine. I'm sure Xavier means nothing by it."

Deacon shook off her hand. "He is disrespecting you, and I won't stand for that."

Xavier took a step closer and poked a finger in Deacon's chest. I moved closer to my friend.

"Deacon, is it? Don't think I answer to you."

"But you answer to me." Perry's voice came from behind us. "Apologize to the lady. Then get your assignment and get on with your day."

"Sorry, Miss Lilian," Xavier said as he swiped some paperwork from her hand.

"This ain't over, Deacon," he growled as he stormed out of the office.

Lilian let out a long breath and melted into her chair.

"Who was that?" I asked.

"Xavier Mack. He's a little rough around the edges, but he's a good inspector," Perry said.

Deacon grunted. "Good, but disrespectful."

"And that's Xavier in a nutshell," Perry agreed.

"Lilian, do you have the copy of the paperwork from the stockyards? For the brand burning that Deacon reported last week?"

She nodded and pulled the paper from a stack on her desk before she handed it to me.

I looked it over. "Should we ride out to Jack Thompson's place to see if he is missing thirty head or more?"

"Exactly. We didn't get to that last week. Derek Gardner agreed to hold the cattle for a few more days until we sort this out."

"Know a man named B. Irving?" I asked. "The name isn't familiar to me."

Deacon shook his head.

"Me either," Perry said. "It is possible he is a foreman I haven't met, but the brand I Bar 8 is not registered, so I suspect it is not real."

"We should publish the brands in a book," Deacon said. "Would be easier for the stockyards to know what is registered and what isn't."

Perry nodded.

"I'll look into that," Lilian said. "We should probably work with Maricopa and Pima Counties on it, too. I'll send off some letters this week."

Then she smiled at Deacon. "That's a great idea. Thanks for sharing it."

When he grinned like a teenager, I rolled my eyes. He was definitely besotted.

As Perry entered his office, Deacon stepped closer to Lilian's desk.

"Why does Xavier call you Valentine?" he asked as he moved the pencil cup around. I smiled when she moved it back. Then he shifted some papers, and she returned them to their original position as she answered him.

"My birthday is on Valentine's Day. He heard my sister say something about it recently."

"Come on, Deacon. We should go," I said. He lingered for a few more seconds before he wished her a good day.

Deacon and I headed out to Jack Thompson's ranch northwest of town, past Chino Valley. It was almost noon by the time we arrived.

Jack Thompson was a kind man, likely in his late forties, with a long blond handlebar mustache. After we introduced ourselves as livestock inspectors, his wife invited us in for the midday meal.

"What brings you out?" he asked.

"You missing any cattle?" I asked.

He frowned. "Yeah. About forty head or so."

Before I continued, I complimented Mrs. Thompson on the meal. She blushed.

"Thirty head came into the Prescott Stockyards last week with some suspicious branding."

"Ever heard of I Bar 8?" Deacon asked. "Or B. Irving?"

"No. That name isn't familiar, and I know most of the owners in the area. The brand sounds odd. Little too close to mine, don't you think?"

I nodded. "We agree. It isn't registered. The brand on the cattle in question appears burned over your brand."

"Mind if we look around?" Deacon asked.

"Please. Anything we can do to help you catch these rustlers."

Deacon turned to Mrs. Thompson and took her hand. "Thank you for the meal, ma'am."

Her face flushed. "You're quite welcome."

As we stepped onto the front porch, I heard her say, "Such nice young men."

Deacon made me proud as he attempted to be more personable.

We followed Jack as he guided us to the barn before we examined his branding iron. Then we inspected a few of his cattle in the corral.

"I'm certain the cattle at the stockyards are yours," Deacon said. "Can you pick them up this week? We'll leave some paperwork in our office with Lilian for you to give to the stockyard manager, Derek Gardner. He will release them to you."

As Jack shook Deacon's hand, I glimpsed a man rounding the corner of the barn. I smiled and shook Jack's hand, despite the unsettling familiarity of the man. His stance reminded me of the man who murdered my mother.

"Your foreman around?" I asked.

"He's out with the herd."

"Any other men staying close to the house today?"

Jack shook his head. "My son's visiting for a few days."

I forced my voice to sound lighter. "Oh? I would have thought he'd join us for lunch."

Jack snorted. "Came home drunk late last night. Don't expect to see him before supper."

"Sorry to hear that. What did you say his name was?"

Deacon shifted from foot to foot as he studied the barn. Then he left while I spoke to Jack.

"Amos. He's a bit of a rowdy one. His mother and I hope he settles down one day."

"Must be hard."

When Deacon came back into sight, I thanked Jack for his cooperation.

"If you see anything suspicious, please send word to the livestock inspection office. Lilian will let us know."

Deacon and I mounted our horses. As we rode back to

town, we discussed our suspicions.

"Someone had been listening outside of the barn," Deacon said. "Saw footprints."

"Yup. Might be the man who murdered my parents."

"Oh, no. I'm sorry, Grady."

"You think he was Thompson's son, Amos?" I asked.

"Not sure. I figure Thompson is around Mama's age. That means his son could be around my age or older."

"About the same age as the man who killed my parents."

Deacon frowned. "Did you get a good look at him?"

"No. Just his back for a few seconds before he ran off. I could be wrong."

"Well, we'll write it up in our report for Perry."

By the time we arrived back in Prescott, it was after five o'clock. We stopped by the office, but Lilian had left for the day. Deacon took a sheet of paper from his notebook and slid a note under the door to let her know Thompson would retrieve his cattle soon.

Then we headed back to the ranch for a late supper. I wanted to tell my sister about our discovery, but it was too soon. I needed more information before I got her hopes up.

The next day, Deacon and I relayed the information we had gathered. Perry suggested we make a trip to the saloons that night. Since Deacon hated the saloons, I told him to go on home and I handled it.

When I entered the Palace, smoke filled the air. I sidled up to the bar and requested a beer and water. After I drank part of the beer, I poured the water into the beer glass to dilute it. I wanted to keep my wits about me.

I struck up a conversation with the bartender. "You know Amos Thompson?"

"Yeah. Comes in fairly often. Was in last night."

"You see him here tonight?"

He nodded toward a young man in his late twenties sitting at a table with a few rough-looking men, nursing his whiskey.

"Who's with him?"

"The young man on his right is Bart Mason."

I sipped my beer. Mason. The man who signed in the I Bar 8 cattle at the stockyards.

"The other man is Caleb Mason. Works for Galen Harper."

I sat up straighter. "Harper, you say?"

"Owns a ranch near Congress. His son, Shane, runs it."

I tossed him a few extra coins before I sat at a table to observe the men without drawing attention.

After a few hours, I gleaned a little information. They celebrated some good fortune. Bart Mason eventually made his way upstairs as Caleb made a big show of paying for the man's entertainment. Amos laughed and drank steadily the entire time. Then Caleb left.

When I walked out the door to follow him, beefy arms grabbed me from behind and shuffled me into an alleyway. Caleb appeared in front of me. He thrust his fist into my gut and I doubled over.

"What's your interest in my party?" he asked.

When I said nothing, he punched me in the face. My skin stung and my eyes burned.

"He asked you a question, boy," the beefy man behind me said.

"Nothing. Was just enjoying a drink alone."

"That so?" Caleb asked. "Then why did you watch every move Thompson made?"

"Who's Thompson?" I asked, doubling down on my story.

Caleb studied my face for a minute. Then he drove his

fist into my gut again. I nearly threw up. It hurt so badly.

"I see you snooping around here again, and it'll be more than my fist that connects with you. You hear me, boy?"

As Caleb walked away, the man holding me lobbed his fist in my face before he shoved me. I never got a good look at him as I fell to the ground. Dirt coated my face while I waited a minute before I stood. My face and stomach ached. Blood trickled down my chin from my nose. I blotted it with my handkerchief. Then I hobbled toward Sunbeam and mounted my horse.

Once I arrived home and cared for my horse, I stumbled into the house. The door slammed against the wall as I lunged toward the table before I collapsed.

"What the... Grady, what happened?"

Deacon rushed to my side and eased me into a chair. "Let me get Mama."

I grabbed his arm. "Don't wake her on my account."

He frowned at me before he dampened a towel and wiped the dirt and dried blood from my face.

"Caleb Mason was the one that did this," I said. "Works for Galen Harper down in Congress."

"Harper? Is that Lilian's father?"

"Dunno, but I plan to ask her about it tomorrow."

Deacon helped me upstairs to my bed. I curled up against the soreness in my gut. As I tried to sleep, my mind worked over everything. Perhaps Caleb Mason was the man I was chasing.

CHAPTER 6

LILIAN

When I arrived at work, Grady and Deacon waited for me to unlock the door. Grady's nose was swollen, and he sported a black eye.

"What happened to you?" I asked.

"Caleb Mason."

The key slipped from my hand and clattered to the floor. My chest constricted as I tried to breathe.

"Are… Are you sure? I've known Caleb for years, and that doesn't seem like something he'd do." I lied.

Grady snorted as Deacon leaned down to pick up the key from the floor. He handed it to me.

"Believe it."

"So you know him?" Deacon asked.

As I debated how much to share, I set my things in a drawer. "He visited my father's ranch often," I blurted out.

Deacon's eyes darkened.

Grady cleared his throat. "So why do you find it hard to believe he beat me up?"

"He's not a violent man."

More lies. I knew him to be frightfully rough. I let out a

slow breath to keep my voice from shaking like my hand did.

Grady glared at me.

"Why did he beat you up?" I asked.

"I looked at him the wrong way. He was hanging out with Amos Thompson and Bart Mason."

"Bart is his brother. I don't know this Thompson man."

Grady placed his hands on my desk and leaned forward as his eyes narrowed. "I think they stole Jack Thompson's cattle."

I frowned. It was entirely possible. My father's associates were not good men. "I see."

As Grady studied me, heat rose from my neck to my forehead. I looked away.

"Hey, Grady, take it easy," Deacon said as he pulled him aside. They whispered before they left for the day.

I sighed as I eased into my chair. Hopefully, they believed my lies.

Then I picked up the papers where I copied the brands. The newspaper agreed to publish the registered brands for the first week after a new registration. That was a tremendous help to me. It gave the public time to review and comment on any brands before we approved them. They also agreed to print a few books for our inspectors and the stockyards throughout the territory.

A few days later, as I finished working on the brand book project, a strange man entered the office. Like Xavier, he wore all black. I gulped as my eyes studied him. He stood nearly six feet five inches, and his thick arms pulled his duster sleeves taut, so much that the seams might split apart.

My throat constricted as I discretely opened the drawer where I kept my pistol. His cold, dark stare frightened me.

"Good afternoon. Can I help you?"

He perused the brands on the wall. "I like how you organized these. Makes it easier to memorize."

Something about the man made me shiver. "Is there something I can help you with, mister?"

He walked the length of the wall of brands, never taking his eyes off them.

"No thank you, Miss Harper."

I shifted in my chair and kept my shaky hand near my open drawer.

"You know me, but what is your name, sir?"

"I know your father." His gaze swept over my face and body in a way that made my skin crawl. "I see some resemblance."

"Is that why you're here? You are an associate of my father?"

He laughed. "No, Miss Harper, I am not here for you."

He returned his gaze to the wall of brands for several minutes.

"If you have no business with the livestock inspectors, then I must ask you to leave," I said as I reached for the pistol.

"No need for that, Miss Harper. I will be on my way now. Tell Thatcher we'll meet soon."

Thatcher? Did he mean Grady?

When I glanced at the clock, it read a quarter 'til five. I grabbed my pistol, other things, and locked up the office early. My sister, Justine, worked at the dry goods store. When I found her, I told her not to hold supper for me.

Then I hurried over to the livery and rented a horse. I mounted the white mare and kicked her into a gallop as I pointed her toward Colter Ranch. I didn't know the way, but Perry said it was impossible to miss the ranch.

After about thirty minutes, I wondered if I had missed it.

Then I crested a hill and saw the massive ranch sprawling in the valley below. Dusk settled over the breathtaking landscape. Two men exited the biggest house on the property. One was big, like Deacon. The other was lanky, like Grady. I pressed the horse forward. When I came closer, they turned around.

"Lilian?" The concern in Deacon's voice softened my heart.

I pulled hard on the reins and dismounted the horse as they jogged toward me.

My breath came in spurts. "Is there... Somewhere to talk?"

Grady took the reins and led the horse to the white house next to the large house. He tied the horse to the post as Deacon held the door open for me.

"Let me make some coffee," Grady said as Deacon offered me a seat at the table.

"Are you alright?" he asked as I set my pistol on the table. He frowned at it. "What happened?"

My voice quavered when I spoke. "A man... At the office. He came in right before closing." I cleared my throat. "He frightened me."

Deacon sat next to me and angled his chair to face me. "Are you alright?"

"I'm... Fine. Just a little shaken."

The warmth of his hands comforted me as he clasped mine in his. Currents coursed through my arms all the way to my heart. He was so close to me I detected a faint scent of orange and cedar on his clothes. My heart sped up again.

"Lil, are you sure?"

Lil? Oh, I liked the nickname he picked for me.

When Grady set the coffee in front of me, Deacon released his hold on my hands. I took a sip and continued my story.

"He studied the brands on the wall. Complimented the order. He knew my name and my father."

Deacon straightened and frowned. His arm jerked like he could leap into action at any moment.

My gaze shifted to Grady across the table. "He knew you too, Grady. He said to tell Thatcher that you'll meet soon. I... I don't know what that means."

Grady's eyes hardened. Deacon's eyes widened as he looked at his friend.

Grady cleared his throat. "Did he wear all black?"

My throat constricted as I dabbed my handkerchief on my forehead.

"Yes, like Xavier does. Except he was massive and more menacing."

Grady looked down.

"Is it him?" Deacon asked.

"Is it who?" I asked.

Grady sighed. "I think so."

"What's going on? Will you tell me? How does he know you, Grady?"

His eyes connected with mine. "I think he is the leader of the gang that murdered my parents six years ago."

The breath left my lungs. I was unaware of his loss. My stomach tightened and my head pounded.

Deacon scooted closer to me and placed an arm around my shoulders. His hand rubbed my arm as I struggled to breathe deeply.

"I'm so sorry," I said. "That must have been terrible."

Grady nodded.

When the silence stretched, I finished the coffee. Then I glanced at the clock. "I should probably go. I wanted you to know in case he came looking for you tonight."

When I stood, Deacon said, "I'll ride with you. It's not safe for you to ride home alone. He could have followed you."

My hand shook as I grabbed my pistol and placed it in the deep pocket of my skirt. I let out a quiet breath and followed Deacon outside.

"I'll come too," Grady said. "There's safety in numbers."

While they saddled their horses, I waited for them in the barn. I watched Deacon's effortless movements. He seemed comfortable there at the ranch. Easygoing. Kind. So different from the first day I met him. Perhaps I misjudged him.

"Ready?" he asked as he checked his revolver for ammunition.

I nodded. He tried to give me a boost up to the horse, but I didn't need his help. When I saw the shocked look on his face, I smiled.

"I grew up on a ranch."

He gave a sharp nod before he mounted his blood bay gelding. Grady mounted his palomino. Then the three of us rode up the lane.

"So," I said as I calmed down. "That's Colter Ranch?"

In the fading light, I could not see it, but I heard the smile in Deacon's voice. "Yeah."

"You'll have to show me around sometime," I said.

He chuckled. "I would like that."

"You two." Grady laughed.

The sound of gunfire startled me. I reached for my pistol. Another shot came from the left. My horse cried out in pain. She reared up. I flew backwards and landed hard on my back. Air whooshed from my lungs.

"Lilian!"

The horse landed with a thud next to me. The wails and moans from it frightened me as she writhed in the dirt.

Another shot kicked up dirt near my arm.

Then a body landed hard on top of me. His weight crushed the air from my lungs. Orange and cedar. Deacon.

He aimed his revolver toward the sound. Then he fired back.

Bullets flew past me.

"Ugh." Deacon's body flinched. Then he carried me in his arms.

"Deacon!" Grady yelled. "Over here!"

Just as we reached the cover of a boulder, Deacon collapsed on top of me. I hit my head. My vision blurred, and I went under.

CHAPTER 7

DEACON

"Lilian!"

My heart lodged in my throat when she fell backwards as her horse reared up. I leaped down from Sergeant and ran toward her. Fire ripped through my side as I sheltered her with my body.

Grady fired back. I did, too.

Another bullet sliced through the skin on my arm. My heart pounded in my ears. We needed cover.

Grady called my name. I swept Lilian up and I raced toward Grady's voice. Pain tore through my calf. I dropped Lilian on the ground. I landed hard on her.

"Lil?"

She didn't respond.

A bullet chipped a piece of rock in my face. It nicked my cheek. I ducked down. The mare's screams pierced the night air. I lifted my pistol and aimed in the general direction of the gunfire.

"I'm out," Grady said.

I angled my hip so he could reload from the bullets on my gun belt. I continued to fire. When he took over, I loaded my pistol again. Then I shifted so my weight was no longer on Lilian. My throat tightened. I hoped she was alright.

Suddenly, horse hooves beat a rhythm away from our position.

"I think they're gone," Grady said as he expelled a loud breath.

"Lil?"

I shook her. She didn't make a sound, and my throat constricted.

The mare wailed. The vet in me wanted to help the horse. But Lilian had to be my priority.

"She's breathing," I said. "I think she hit her head."

Grady walked over to the mare. "You got any bullets left?"

"Yup."

"We gotta put this horse down."

"Grady, no," I whined. No way would I kill her.

"Deacon." His voice held a warning.

I gritted my teeth as I pushed through the pain to stand. I knew Grady and I could help the horse. We were veterinarians. Surely, we could help.

"You do it or give me your gun, and I will."

As I hobbled over to the horse, I let out a guttural moan. Then I whispered soft words to the horse as I pulled the trigger. Tears burned my eyes. I was supposed to save lives, not take them.

"It had to be done," Grady said. He slapped me on the shoulder. "Let's take care of Lilian."

Despite the fire burning my side and the pain in my calf, I limped over to Lilian after I holstered my gun.

As night fell upon us, I dropped to my feet. My hands felt her for signs of injury. "I think she just hit her head.

Help me get her up on my horse."

I groaned as I lifted her and carried her toward my horse. Grady held Sergeant steady. Then I mounted the horse as Grady stood ready to catch her if she slipped from my arms. I settled her against my chest and held her tight. Her legs draped over my right leg. Strange feelings stirred as I relished her nearness.

Grady mounted his horse, and we rode toward town. When we were still far off, Lilian stirred. I let out a long breath.

"What happened?" she asked as she sat up.

"Stay still. I've got you."

Her hair brushed against my cheek as she tried to move. It felt soft against my skin.

"Woman. Be still."

"Woman?" her voice held an edge.

I tightened my hold on her. "You're safe, but I'd rather you not fall off my horse with all your squirming." And I wanted to hold her longer.

"Oh."

She lifted her arm and placed it around my neck. Lavender drifted up to my nose. I inhaled deeply as she leaned against my chest. She placed her other hand on the horn of the saddle. My heart thrummed faster than a galloping horse. She felt so perfect resting against me. I wanted the moment to last.

"Where do you live?" I asked. My voice sounded strange to my ears.

She gave me directions, and I pointed Sergeant that way.

When we arrived, her sisters flung the door open.

"Lilian, what happened?"

Lilian slid down from my horse into their waiting arms, leaving mine feeling empty. She started toward the house.

Then she stopped and glanced over her shoulder.

"You coming?"

My heart raced as I desperately wanted to accept her invitation. I cleared my throat. "I'm fine."

"So you're just gonna bleed all over your horse?"

Grady dismounted and tugged on my arm. When I dismounted on my bad leg, I collapsed onto the ground.

"I got you," Grady said as he helped me up. "Lean on me."

He looped his arm around my waist while Lilian held the door open.

"Hayley, get my kit," she instructed her sister. "Justine, hot water."

Her lovely blue eyes softened as she "tsked" at me.

"You're a mess. Sit."

Her warm hand gently pressed my chest as she held out a chair. I fell into it.

When she yanked on my shirt, my mouth went dry.

"What are you doing?" I growled.

"Fixing you." She smirked and muttered. "Fixing."

The word I used the day I met her. I gave her a half smile.

Then I took off my shirt. When she glared at me, I took off my undershirt as well.

Her eyes roamed over my bare chest, leaving behind a trail of fire until they rested on my side. She frowned.

"You need stitches."

Then she sat down next to me as she placed my arm on the back of her chair. Her hair was loose from her fall and it brushed against my skin. I held my breath and closed my eyes for a moment.

"Hayley, can you look at his calf?"

I propped it on the other chair next to me.

"Relax, Deacon," Lilian said. "I will not hurt you."

I wouldn't feel the pain, anyway. Not with her so close and distracting me.

She tilted her head as she studied the wound on my side. Then she took a damp cloth and wiped away the blood. Her sister cut my pant leg open and cleaned my calf.

"This is just a graze," Hayley said. "Not sure you could stitch it."

Lilian stood and leaned over me. The air sizzled as her hair brushed against my bare chest. I sucked in a sharp breath, which made my side sear in pain before I gritted my teeth.

"Yeah, I see what you mean."

When she sat down again, I reached for her hair and slid it over her far shoulder.

"Sorry." Her cheeks bloomed red as her eyes darted away.

"Justine, can you pour some whiskey for Deacon?"

No one answered. I looked around the room. Justine was deep in conversation with Grady, who smiled like a schoolboy. I rolled my eyes.

"Hayley?"

She stood and brought me a glass.

"Drink up, Mr. Colter," Lilian teased. "When I start sewing, you'll be glad for it."

The drink burned my gut almost as much as her touch burned my skin. Hayley poured me another glass, and I sipped it.

"All of it," Lilian commanded.

"Are you trying to get me drunk?" I asked as I searched her blue eyes.

"What would make you think that?"

I downed the second glass. The tension unwound from

my muscles as the drink went to my head. Lilian leaned over my side and held the threaded needle. When she pierced my skin, I inhaled sharply through my nose.

"Hayley, this one is tougher than he looks. Give him another one."

"I don't—"

"Deacon, do it."

I downed the third glass of fire. My head swam, and I suddenly felt as hot as the fire we used during branding season.

As she stitched up my side, I relaxed. My hand brushed her silky cheek. She looked so beautiful as she bit her lower lip while she pulled the thread taut.

My eyes studied the side of her face. She had a freckle near the corner of her left eye. Other lighter freckles dusted her sweet, rosy cheeks.

"There. Done."

She stood abruptly and tossed me my undershirt. "Put this back on. Then I'll look at your arm."

She fanned her face while I took my sweet time putting my shirt on. It took everything within me not to pull her onto my lap and capture her lips with mine. Certainly, they must taste like honey.

Lilian reached for my arm. She took the damp cloth and wiped away the blood. Then she snorted. "Oh, this is just a minor scratch. It'll be fine."

"Now let me see... Your..." Her voice dropped to a whisper. "Face."

I placed a hand on her waist and drew her closer. Then I turned my cheek toward her, without releasing my hold. I enjoyed the feel of her waist under my fingertips.

"Um..." Her breathing shallowed. She took the cloth and slowly dabbed it on my cheek. Then my lip. Then down my neck.

I pulled her so close her breath tickled my cheek.

Her hand froze. Her eyes locked with mine. Boy, did I want to kiss her.

"How's our patient?" Grady's voice broke the moment.

Lilian recovered and twisted out of my hold. "Fine. Just fine."

The last word was a little sultry. I smiled as I savored the effect I had on her.

———

GRADY

"Justine? That's a lovely name," I said, when I was certain Lilian didn't need my help with Deacon.

"Thank you," she said as she took my arm and led me to a chair in the parlor.

I sat and kept one eye on Deacon, who took off both his shirt and undershirt. He looked very uncomfortable.

"How long have you lived in Prescott?" I asked the beautiful Justine.

She smiled, and her brown eyes lit up. "Just a few months. As soon as Lilian hired on at the livestock inspection office, she sent for me and Hayley."

I quirked an eyebrow. "Where did you live before?"

"Our family's ranch down near Congress. The three of us were ready to leave. With Papa, one never knew if we would feast like queens or beg like paupers. Since we're old enough to marry, we thought we ought to move where there was opportunity."

I glanced over at Deacon as he downed a glass of whiskey. He seemed to relax a little.

When I turned my attention back to Justine, I observed details about her. Her blond hair hung in a braid down her back. I wondered if she normally wore it that way or only in the evening when they weren't expecting company. She pulled it over her shoulder and played with the tip.

"How about you?" she asked.

I cleared my throat. "I moved here about six years ago, when I was fifteen. My sister married Deacon's older brother. After my parents were murdered, I moved to live with her at Colter Ranch."

"Oh, I'm so sorry for your loss." She reached over and squeezed my hand.

My eyes locked with hers as her touch sent waves of warmth through me. When she quickly withdrew her hand, I was certain she felt it, too.

"Perhaps with this new job at the livestock inspection office, I'll finally find the rustlers that did it."

We talked for several minutes more. Then I stood.

"Go to dinner with me on Friday?" I asked. "Maybe we could invite Deacon and Lilian?"

Justine glanced down. Then she looked back up and smiled. "I would like that."

I stepped closer and took her hand in mine. Then I placed a kiss on the top of it. Her smile grew bigger. Then her eyes widened as she looked over my shoulder.

"Um, I think you need to rescue my sister."

I swiveled around in time to see Deacon pull Lilian closer. I dropped Justine's hand. The look in his eyes spurred my feet forward.

"Just how much liquor did you give him?" I asked.

Deacon dropped his hold on Lilian.

"Three glasses."

"Well, I guess that explains why he's so… My apologies, Lilian. I should get him home."

She nodded as she stepped away from him.

"Come on." I placed my arm around Deacon's waist.

"See you tomorrow, Lil." I cringed as his words slurred.

Then I bid the Harper sisters farewell as I helped Deacon out to his horse. He mounted it without issue.

"Try to stay on top of your horse, buddy," I said as I grabbed Sergeant's reins.

I mounted Sunbeam while I kept a hold on Sergeant's reins. Then I led the way home. Surely, Deacon would be embarrassed the next time he saw Lilian.

CHAPTER 8

JUSTINE

As I closed the door behind the handsome Grady Thatcher, I turned my attention to my sister.

"How are you, Lilian? What happened, anyway?"

"I think I hit my head. I'm a little sore, but I don't think they shot me."

She told me the entire story as I examined her. When I didn't find any noteworthy injuries, I made her some willow bark tea. Then I sat across from her.

"Grady's life is in danger?" I asked as I frowned.

"I think so. The shooters may have been after me, Deacon, Grady, or all of us. They did not hurt Grady?"

I shook my head.

"Well, maybe they were after me. Could have been the man that came to the office."

"I think you should have someone walk you home from now on. At least until things settle down."

She sipped the tea. "I suppose Deacon would be happy to walk me home." She fanned her face at the mention of his name.

"He was pretty easy on the eyes," Hayley said. "All of

him." She giggled.

Lilian frowned at her.

"You like him," I said.

Lilian shook her head. "No. No. I work with him."

I smiled. "You do. Look at your face. You can't muster any sternness as you try to deny it."

She sipped more of the tea as her cheeks turned rosy.

"And you," Hayley said as she turned to me. "You are smitten with Grady."

My face flushed, so I could not deny it. "He invited me to have supper on Friday night. He thought Deacon might want to bring you, Lilian."

"What? Oh, no." Her mussed hair bounced as she shook her head.

I rolled my eyes at her continued denial. The spark between the two of them was obvious even before she plied him with alcohol. After? Well, I think it turned up to a full flame, at least for him.

"I don't suppose they have a younger, equally handsome friend, do they?" Hayley asked as she leaned forward with eyes full of hope.

"Not that I know of," Lilian said.

Hayley let out a long breath as she sagged against the chair back. "Well, it looks like I have a dinner date with myself on Friday."

"Are you sure, Hay? I could ask Grady if we can bring you."

She snorted. "That would be awkward. I'll just read a book and dream of my future man." She giggled. "The two of you found someone special already."

I certainly was looking forward to seeing Grady Thatcher again with his brown eyes and sandy hair. He was the sweetest, gentlest man of my acquaintance.

The flutters he stirred in my stomach would keep him in my mind. Yes, I eagerly looked forward to Friday.

———

LILIAN

As I climbed into bed, I reflected on those moments with Deacon. His touch unnerved me and excited me at the same time. Surely, he was going to kiss me. When Grady interrupted us, I was a little sad. A kiss from Deacon Colter might be nice.

After having seen more of him than I should have, it'd be hard to look him in the eye at work. I tossed onto my other side. It was the right decision. I had to patch up his side.

I sighed. I suppose I could have asked him to hold his shirt up. But his arm would have been so close to me. No. It was the right call. Maybe.

I rolled onto my back and stared at the ceiling. When did I start to care for him? Maybe it was when he saved my life. The way he called out my name reverberated in my ears. His tone sounded like a man who feared the worst fate for his loved one. Pained. Fearful. Heartbroken.

Or maybe it was when he stood up to Xavier for me. When he defended me that day, he wasn't fighting for any woman's honor. It was personal. He fought for *my* honor.

I sighed and flopped onto my side as sleep eluded me. I ought to close my eyes. Let sleep wipe away his look of intense desire from my mind.

The next morning, I woke up late and rushed through

my morning routine. I hurried out the door and collided with the man who sweetened my dreams.

"Morning, Lil," he said. "Happy birthday."

My cheeks warmed. "Morning."

"Thought you might like company on the way to work."

My heart raced as Deacon fell into step beside me. The smell of his shaving soap wafted toward me. Clean. Manly.

"I'm sorry for being too forward with you last night. I don't drink. Ever. Saw what it's done to my younger brother. So, after three drinks, I wasn't myself."

I glanced over at him. He refused to make eye contact with me, and his gaze remained focused forward.

"Apology accepted," I said as I looped my hand around his arm. His lips twitched when he fought against a smile.

"Thank you for walking me to work."

"Any time."

When we came into view of the office, I released my hold. Grady leaned against the outside of the building. He pushed away as I stepped onto the porch.

"You ask her?" he asked.

Deacon cleared his throat. "Would you go to supper with me on Friday? And Grady and Justine?"

"A double date," Grady stated.

When I turned to face Deacon, his eyes darted away, and he cleared his throat. His hand patted his leg. His nervousness softened my heart.

"Yes, I would love to. Now, we best get started with our workday."

I unlocked the door and entered the office. After I stowed my things in my desk, I opened the curtains to let more light in. Deacon hovered near my desk.

"I have something for you." He dug around in his pocket and pulled out three wooden items before he held out his hand.

After I accepted the blocks of wood, I turned them over. One had the shape of a cow, another a horse, and the last a sheep. I smiled.

"This isn't a birthday gift. It's only coincidence that I brought them today."

"Thank you."

He took one back. "See, you can ink it on the flat surface and then press it on paper and…" He shifted from one foot to the other. Then he thrust the block back into my hand.

I laughed. "I like them. Thank you. I will update our brand wall soon."

Grady stepped forward. "If the two of you are finished…" He nodded to Deacon, who ducked into Perry's office and sat at a desk.

"Would you mind searching the book of sketches for the man you saw yesterday?" he asked.

Once I sat down at my desk, Grady placed the book in front of me. I opened it and studied each face carefully. After I flipped through a few, Grady joined Deacon in Perry's office. I continued looking through the pictures until my eyelids grew heavy. Coffee would clear my mind, so I stood and heated water on the stove.

"I took care of the horse this morning," Deacon said from behind me. "I spoke with the livery owner."

"You didn't have to do that. It was my fault."

"I brought him a replacement from my uncle's stables. He's a breeder and trainer."

"Oh. How much do I owe you?"

He shook his head.

"I can pay you back."

He smiled at me. "It's unnecessary. I was the one that

pulled the trigger, so I made it right."

I held up a mug, and he nodded.

"Any luck with the sketches?" he asked. Then he took the coffee from my hands.

"Not yet. Here." I handed him another mug. "For Grady."

He thanked me and returned to Perry's office.

After I poured myself a cup of coffee, I returned to my desk. A few minutes later, I flipped to a sketch that looked frightfully familiar.

"Deacon, Grady!"

My heart lodged in my throat as I pointed to the page. They stood over my desk. "This is the man that was here yesterday."

I turned the book around so they could study the sketch. A shadow settled on Grady's face. His jaw twitched. Then he turned on his heel and stormed out of the building.

"Deacon, what's going on?" I asked.

"You just identified the man who murdered his parents. Is there a name?"

I shook my head.

"Mind if I borrow this?"

When I nodded, he took the page and left the building.

Neither of them returned until later in the day. Deacon handed me the sketch back, and I placed it in the book.

"The sheriff knew nothing other than he's wanted for rustling and murder."

I swallowed the lump in my throat as the realization hit me hard. I stared down a murderer in that very office just yesterday.

CHAPTER 9

DEACON

As the week wore on, we made little progress investigating the identity of the man who shot at us. Grady talked about visiting the saloon again, but I warned him not to because of what happened last time.

When Friday afternoon arrived, Perry allowed us to leave early since he heard about our double date.

"Thanks, Perry," Lilian said. "Deacon, would you mind walking me home? I want to change into something nicer."

I frowned. She looked perfect already. Grady jabbed me in the ribs.

"Take her home and meet me at the dry goods store," Grady said. "I'm gonna see if Justine can leave early, too."

As I walked Lilian home, I realized I kept rubbing my thumb over my index finger, so I stuffed my hand in my pocket. Nothing like scaring her off before the date even started.

"What time should I pick you up?" I asked.

"About an hour."

I opened my pocket watch. "So at five forty-seven?"

She laughed. "Around then."

As I walked toward the dry goods store, I realized she thought I was joking. I wasn't. She didn't know me well enough to understand I was dead serious. When she did, I hoped she would still be interested.

"Deacon, welcome!" Justine greeted me as I entered the store. "Is Lilian home?"

I nodded.

Justine gave Grady a kiss on the cheek, then she bounded out the door.

"Lil said to meet them at five forty-seven," I told him.

Grady slapped me on the back. "I'll bet. So, did you purchase a birthday present for her?"

My stomach squeezed tight and sweat dotted my forehead. "Should I have?"

He studied me for a moment. "It might be too early. This is our first date and all. Then again, it'd impress her if you did."

"I wouldn't know what to get her," I said as my foot caught on the threshold of the dry goods store. Instinctively, Grady grabbed my arm.

"Careful."

Heat warmed my neck and face as I followed him across the street to the flower shop.

"Think about what you might get your mother or Vi for their birthday."

I snorted. A dime novel didn't sound all that exciting. That's what Vi would like. Mama would appreciate a trinket.

As Grady picked out flowers, he handed me a bouquet. "These would be perfect for Lilian."

"Wait. I should get her flowers and a gift?" I rubbed my thumb across my index finger as my chest tightened.

"The flowers are for your first date. The gift is for her

birthday."

As I paid for the blossoms, I sighed heavily. I ought to be grateful for Grady's help, but I felt annoyed instead.

"I guess I'll go shop for something, then."

With a bouquet in hand, I left. I felt silly carrying it from store to store. Finally, at the third store, I confessed to the clerk that I needed some help.

"I'm looking for a birthday gift for my…"

My words faded away. I didn't want to call Lilian my sweetheart. It was only our first date. Coworker sounded too insignificant.

The clerk raised an eyebrow.

After I cleared my throat, I said, "My girl."

The entire situation weighed heavily on my mind. A four-hour surgery to extract a bullet from a horse would have been easier than trying to figure out how to court Lilian. I only wanted to be myself, but I guess I wasn't impressive enough.

"Perhaps earrings? Or a lovely broach?" the clerk suggest-ed.

As I pictured Lilian at the office, I could not recall her wearing earrings or a broach or jewelry of any kind. I did not know what she liked.

Swallowing the lump in my throat, I said, "Earrings."

The clerk showed me a wide variety of earrings. Clearly, I was in over my head. I sighed and thought for a few minutes. Lilian acted practical, like Mama, so maybe something pretty but modest.

There was a pair of dangling pearl earrings. Simple, yet elegant, so I pointed to them. "I'll take those. Do you have a nice little box for them?"

The clerk nodded. Then he gave me the total. Uncertain if five dollars was too much, I compared it to the price of the last pair of boots I bought. I paid six dollars for them. Since I had the money, I thrust it at the clerk. He handed me the box, and I stuffed it in my pocket.

When I exited the store, Grady said, out of breath, "There you are. We're going to be late. Come on."

He tugged on my arm and I followed his brisk pace to the Harper girls' place. When Grady knocked on the door, Hayley opened it and invited us inside.

"They are almost ready."

"See," I muttered to Grady. "We aren't late."

He glared at me.

Justine entered the room first. Grady cleared his throat. It was the first time I noticed him acting nervously around someone.

"You look lovely," he said as he handed her a bouquet. "Lovely flowers for a lovely lady."

I refrained from rolling my eyes. He was smooth, and it seemed to work, judging by the pink gracing Justine's cheeks.

When Lilian entered the main room, my breath caught. She appeared striking in her bright blue silk dress. It brought out the blue of her eyes and made her strawberry blond hair appear even redder. Her ivory skin looked silky. When I pictured her wearing the earrings with that dress, I felt better about my choice.

After I cleared my throat, I stepped forward. Right as I shoved the flowers toward her, she moved closer and they smacked her in the face. My face heated so hot I thought my skin might burn off.

"Oh, I'm sorry," I said. "Are you alright?"

She laughed and accepted the flowers. "I suppose that's one way to make sure I smell them."

She winked at me, and I breathed a little easier.

Grady coughed and said under his breath, "Compliment her."

"You look nice."

He shook his head as Justine arranged the flowers in separate vases.

"I mean, you look beautiful, Lil."

She glanced down as rosy circles appeared on the apples of her cheeks. That little freckle by the corner of her left eye grew on me, too. It was cute but figured I ought to keep that opinion to myself.

When I offered her my arm, she took it, and I steered her out of the house.

"You kids have fun!" Hayley teased as she closed the door behind us.

"Sorry we didn't invite your sister."

"Don't worry about Hay," Lilian replied. "She planned to curl up by the fire with a good book."

At least three times before we reached the restaurant, I patted my jacket pocket to ensure I hadn't lost the gift. I didn't know when I should give it to her.

Once we arrived, the hostess seated us right away. I liked the place Grady picked out. They laid out the tables in a symmetrical pattern, which instantly helped me relax. Polished dark wood panels covered the walls, which gave the room a very sophisticated appeal. I felt a little underdressed in my denim pants and white button-down shirt.

After we ordered, but before our meal arrived, I pulled the tiny box from my pocket and I slid it over to Lilian.

"Happy birthday." I flashed what I hoped was a charming smile.

"You didn't have to buy me anything," she whispered.

"Of course he didn't," Justine nudged her. "But he did, and it shows how thoughtful he is."

In that moment, I wondered if Grady and Justine con-spire-ed to help me win over Lilian. I didn't mind, as I needed all the guidance I could get.

When she opened the box, her breath caught. She placed a hand over her heart. Tears pooled in her eyes.

My throat constricted and my shoulders slumped. "You don't like it. I can take it back—"

She pressed a finger on my lips. I wanted to glance away, as I was positive she hated the gift.

"I love it," she whispered as she dabbed the corner of her eyes with her handkerchief. "They are beautiful."

The smile on her lips reflected in her eyes. She leaned over and kissed my cheek. As I tried to calm my racing heart, she showed the gift to her sister.

"So expensive," Justine commented. "And lovely."

Someone nudged my foot under the table. I glanced at Grady and he winked. He mouthed the word "nice."

I let out a slow breath. Maybe I picked the right gift af-ter all.

"Put them on," Justine suggested.

Lilian looked at me. "Should I?"

I nodded, since I wanted to see them with that dress.

She took them out of the box and placed one on each earlobe. The jewelry added the perfect finishing touch as the pearls danced with each movement of her head.

"What do you think?" she asked me.

"I think you make them look even prettier."

Her cheeks turned rosy as she squeezed my hand. When she tried to pull it away, I held on and we held hands until the food arrived. Relief washed over me. Perhaps I came across better than I thought.

———

GRADY

All my scheming with the jubilant Justine may have been unnecessary. When Deacon handed Lilian the gift, his timing was perfect. Justine winked at me. I placed my hand on hers.

When I saw Deacon's gift for Lilian, I nearly choked. It was expensive, especially for recently having met Lilian. Then I caught the joy in her eyes, and I realized the price mattered little. Without intending to, Deacon totally secured her heart with that one simple, expensive gift.

After I kicked his foot, he looked at me, and I mouthed the word "nice". He looked ready to run away. I knew he wasn't the best at understanding people, much less women, so I made it my personal mission to encourage him.

Justine leaned over next to me. "Deacon set the bar high. My birthday is in April."

Warmth spread through my middle as I whispered to her, "I accept your challenge. And I like you see us still together in April."

"Oh, Grady, I have no plans to let you get away."

As her smile softened her words, my gaze shifted to her. She was breathtaking in that pale pink dress with her blond hair fixed so perfectly. Honey-colored ringlets cascaded down her back. I could have kissed her right there if the server wasn't setting out our meal.

Justine and I carried the conversation during the meal, as I figured we would. As soon as Deacon and Lilian finished eating, he took her hand again. I was happy for him.

After we ate some dessert, it was time to take the lovely Harper sisters home. The evening air chilled, but I barely noticed it as Justine and I whispered. She continued to weave her way deeper into my heart.

One block away from the restaurant, a man stepped out of the shadows.

"Well, if it isn't the infamous Grady Thatcher." The man spat at my feet.

I released Justine and positioned her behind me. My heart nearly stopped when Lilian spoke.

"Caleb," she said his name with disdain.

"Lilian and Justine Harper. You should be careful about the company you keep."

"Deacon, take the ladies home," I said as I stepped closer to Caleb Mason. His height and size didn't bother me. He could probably best me, but protectiveness rose in me. I just wanted Justine and Lilian away from him. Much to my dismay, Lilian stepped forward.

"Leave us alone, Caleb."

Deacon flinched.

When Caleb grabbed Lilian's arm, Deacon lunged forward until I stepped in his path.

"Let her go!" Deacon growled out the words.

"You heard the man," I echoed. "Your dispute is with me, not them."

Caleb released Lilian's arm and pushed her toward Deacon as he laughed. "You know nothing about the beef I have with her."

When Deacon took another step toward him, I asked him again to take the girls home. "I'll be along in a minute."

As soon as they were out of sight, I grabbed Caleb's shirt collar and dragged him into the closest alleyway.

"What do you want?"

He laughed. His breath heated my face as he brushed my hands away from his shirt.

"You don't know who shot at you and that hussy, do

you?"

"What are you talking about?"

"Those bullets weren't for your friend. They were meant for you."

I pinned him against the wall with my forearm on his throat. "You better leave the Harper sisters alone."

He spat in my face.

I shoved him one more time, then I stepped back and wiped the spit from my cheek.

"You don't know what this is about." He snorted. "We aren't done with you. It's taken us a long time to find you."

After I backed out of the alleyway, I turned toward the Harper home.

"You're on notice, Thatcher! Clock is ticking. Enjoy the short time you have left with Justine."

I bristled but continued on my way. By the time I reached Justine's house, I settled enough to enjoy the rest of the evening, even though Caleb's words still rang in my ears.

CHAPTER 10

JUSTINE

After Lilian opened the door to our house, I asked, "What does Caleb want with Grady? How do they even know each other?"

"A few weeks ago, we were chasing down a lead on the rustlers that burned over the Thompson cattle brand," Deacon said. "Grady went to a saloon to find Amos Thompson. He was hanging out with Caleb and Bart Mason."

"Wait, Bart is involved too?" I asked.

"Not sure," Deacon said. "I worked with Bart at the stock-yards. Seemed like a nice young man."

Lilian offered Deacon a spot on the couch, but he remained standing while I paced the length of the parlor.

Hayley joined us. "What happened?"

Lilian filled her in.

"I don't understand why Caleb would care that Grady saw him with Amos Thompson," Lilian said.

As I wondered what dark thing Grady stumbled into, I wrung my hands together. I never did like Caleb. Not when he courted Lilian. Not when he came to the ranch. He always frightened me.

A knock sounded on the door. I rushed to it, but Deacon stopped me.

"Sit. I'll get it."

When he opened it, Grady entered, and I hurried to his side. "Are you alright?"

"Yup."

After I led him to a chair, I fixed iced tea for each of us.

"How well do you know Caleb?" Grady asked Lilian, as his eyebrows furrowed.

When she looked away, I didn't blame her. It was a painful topic for her.

"He courted her at Papa's request," I said. "He was a terrible match for her. Unfortunately, Papa convinced him there could be a future with her."

"Justine, please," Lilian said, as tears pooled in her eyes.

"We must tell them what kind of man Caleb is."

Her hands shook until she wrapped them around her middle. Then she gave me a slight nod.

"When Lilian resisted his advances…"

Deacon shifted on the couch next to Lilian. He placed an arm around her shoulders. Grady observed her while I continued.

"At first, it was bruises easily hidden. Then it was cuts on her face."

Deacon's jaw twitched.

"And, well, more sinister deeds." I could not divulge everything. She needed to decide when and how she shared her darkest secret.

Her face went pale, and she shook. Even when Deacon held her close, she remained ramrod straight on the couch.

I sighed loudly to draw the attention away from her.

"Anyway, she broke off the relationship and us girls decided it was time to leave the ranch. None of us trusted Papa to find a suitable husband for us. His friends were not the type of men we wanted to marry."

Lilian cleared her throat. "So, I moved here first and got the job at the livestock inspection office. Once I could afford this place, I sent for my sisters."

When she spoke about us, she relaxed. My heart ached. I had hoped her past would not follow us to Prescott, and she'd left it behind forever.

Grady ran a hand through his hair. "I get the sense that Caleb's issue is with me and not you."

Deacon frowned.

"What do you mean?" I asked.

"I think he's connected to the theft of Thompson's cattle or…"

Deacon cleared his throat. "Your parents."

Grady nodded grimly.

"He claimed the shooter was after me, not Lilian or Deacon."

"The man in black," Lilian said. "He declared he would meet Grady soon. You mentioned he looks like the man who murdered your parents."

I reached over for Grady's hand. His eyes narrowed, and a shadow fell over his face.

"Enough about work." He straightened and plastered a smile on his face. "Let's not leave such a somber end to a wonderful date."

I giggled. "Was it wonderful?"

He stood and grabbed his empty glass before ushering me to the kitchen. Once he set it by the sink, he pulled me into his arms.

"The night would be wonderful if you'd let me kiss you, Justine."

I grinned before he leaned down and his lips tasted mine

for a minute.

"Go on a picnic with me tomorrow?" he whispered as his hands remained at my waist.

"What if it is overcast and cold?" I teased.

"Then I'll have to think about how to keep you warm."

Before I could respond, he lowered his lips to mine. The warm kiss invited me to press closer. As I returned the kiss, I slid my hands up his chest and rested them behind his neck. He deepened the kiss, sending pleasant waves through my limbs. I was most definitely falling for Grady Thatcher. When he ended the kiss, I brushed my lips across his one more time before I smirked.

"I see how you might," I said.

"Hmm?"

"Keep me warm. I would love to picnic with you. Will it be just us?"

"Of course."

The idea of having him all to myself for a few hours pleased me.

———

LILIAN

What started as a perfect evening with the perfect gift turned dark after we ran into Caleb Mason. The evil man. He ruined everything good in my life.

When Justine began telling Deacon and Grady about him, I stiffened. I prayed she would not reveal the worst of it. What she shared was bad enough.

After we talked about Caleb, Grady and Justine moved to the kitchen to steal a few kisses. I was happy for her. Our dream was that she and Hayley find honorable men. Grady embodied it.

Hayley excused herself and returned to her room.

"Lil, what happened?" Deacon asked softly.

My eyes burned at the question. If he only knew. He would not have given me those earrings or flowers or taken me out for a delightful date. He would run far away from me.

"It's alright. I won't ask." He caressed my arm as he rested his on my shoulders.

"Do you like the earrings?"

"Yes. Very much. But I think you spent too much on me."

He beamed. "I don't think so. Especially not if you love them."

"I do. Thank you."

"Lil?"

"Hmm?"

"Can I kiss you?"

My heart pounded against my rib cage. I scooted away from him. Part of me wanted him to kiss me. Instead, I should lock myself in my room and not come out for a year.

"I... I'm sorry," he murmured. "Reading people... I'm no good at it."

He stood abruptly and rushed to the door.

I stood and followed him. When I touched his arm, he stopped, but he didn't face me.

"Deacon," I whispered. "I'm the one who is sorry. Please, look at me."

When he faced me, I recognized the pain and fear in his eyes. Fear of rejection. How could such a confident, kind man could fear rejection?

"I'm still leery after what I experienced with Caleb. It's

not you. You are a good man. I…" I sighed. "Tonight, spending time with you… I want to see you again."

His eyes grew hopeful.

"I'm just—"

"Wounded."

As tears burned my eyes, I glanced elsewhere.

Then he placed his hand on my neck and leaned down. His lips brushed featherlight over mine before he released me.

"I understand."

"Please be patient with me."

He trailed his fingers down my arm. "Happy birthday, Lil. I'll see you soon."

After he nodded toward his friend, Grady slowly extracted himself from my sister's arms.

Then we bid our men farewell. My heart claimed Deacon already. I just needed to get my mind to agree.

CHAPTER II

GRADY

As Deacon and I rode home, my mind churned. I wished it was over thoughts of the sweet Justine. Instead, Caleb's words disturbed me.

"He said it took them too long to find me," I said into the silence.

"Were those his exact words?" Deacon asked.

Sunbeam snorted, and I patted his neck.

"Yup."

"Grady, I've known you a long time now. As a young man, I doubt you did something that caused men to hunt you down. Save one thing."

"Witness my parents' murder." My stomach clenched as the bleak reality settled over me.

"The man in black, Caleb Mason, and Amos Thompson must be in the same gang."

Even in the dark, the peace of the ranch filled my soul. A million stars sparkled overhead. The moonlight glistened off the lake in the valley below. The soft glow of lamplight shone from the bunkhouse, the ranch house, and the small house.

We kicked our horses into a trot until we arrived at the barn. Then we dismounted and lit two lanterns while we took care of them. After we extinguished the lanterns, we walked to our house.

"Why would they care after all this time?" I asked.

"The man in black knows you can identify him. The only reason Caleb would care is if he was associated with him. It's the only thing that makes sense."

"So how do we find them and stop them before they come after me or hurt someone close to me?"

Deacon let out a long breath. "We must learn everything the Harper sisters know about the Masons."

"Justine and Hayley attend church on Sunday. Justine said she'd convince Lilian to go. Let's invite them to the ranch for Sunday supper."

"That would give us plenty of time to ask questions. You're gifted at drawing information from a person without them knowing you're doing it."

I snorted as I pushed the door of our house open. Deacon lit a lamp. Then he built a fire in the fireplace.

"I'll talk to Ellie Mae tomorrow. I'm sure we could squeeze the Harper sisters around the table. Especially if James, Boone, and Jaclyn aren't visiting."

I sank into my favorite chair and rubbed my hands on my knees.

"Seems like things are serious between you and Justine," Deacon said as he sat facing the fire.

"We're picnicking tomorrow."

He grinned. "Judging by the way your lips locked with hers, she's excited to go."

"Yes. Now I wonder if it's a good idea. What if Caleb or his friends are watching me or the Harpers?"

His smile faded. "Maybe you should pick a public place.

Could you picnic at the courthouse plaza?"

I frowned. "I had hoped for something secluded."

Deacon stood and squeezed my shoulder. "You're the only one that can decide what is safest. Night."

Then he strode into his bedroom.

I remained staring into the fire for a while before I retired to my room upstairs.

The next morning, I lingered after breakfast at my sister's house.

"Something on your mind, Grady?" Sam asked.

"Need to talk to my sister for a minute."

"Come on Sterling, Brody. Let's go out to the barn."

"Barn! Barn!" Brody repeated as Sam leaned down and picked up his toddler while four-year-old Sterling took his hand. Once they left, the house sounded strangely quiet. Even Baby Ashley slept in the bassinet nearby.

Ellie Mae poured me more coffee, and she refilled her mug before she sat across from me.

"First, do you mind if Deacon and I invite the three Harper sisters for Sunday supper tomorrow?"

"Three? I'm not sure I know the Harper sisters."

I sighed. "Lilian is the secretary at the livestock inspection office. She's the one Deacon likes."

"Oh?" Her eyes lit with excitement.

"Justine—"

"Ah, she's caught your eye." She beamed.

"How can you tell?"

"It's written all over your face as you say her name."

I rubbed my hand on my pants. "I am taking her on a picnic in a few hours."

"I see. And the third sister?"

"Hayley is the youngest. Doesn't seem right to send her to an empty house after church. I'm hoping you and Vi will entertain her while her sisters disappear for a bit."

Ellie Mae laughed. "Of course. Please stay in sight of the house."

"Yes, Sis."

I sipped my coffee for a bit.

"Was there something else on your mind?"

"The farm."

The light left her face, and she stared out the window.

"I want to sell it."

Her head snapped back to me. "Are you certain?"

"It's time. I've chosen my career as a vet and now as a livestock inspector. Eventually, I'll be a vet again. I have no interest in farming."

"When do you want to travel to Chino Valley to complete the sale?"

"I was thinking early April, so we get past any chance of snow."

"Alright. I don't think Sam can leave with everything going on here. Maybe Vi and Hannah can help with the children. Can Deacon come with us?"

"I'm sure he will. We want to investigate the murder."

Her eyes went wide.

"We have a sketch of the gang's leader, except we don't know his name yet."

She looked down at her coffee and said nothing for several minutes.

"After all this time..." Her voice faded. Then she sat up straighter. "You stay safe, Grady. I could not bear to lose you, too."

I rounded the table and gave her a hug.

"I'll do my best."

She sniffled as I left.

A pang of guilt rooted in my heart. I knew I shocked her

with my sudden announcement. Probably should have eased her into the idea of selling the farm.

Around ten, I saddled Sunbeam and headed to town. I decided Deacon's suggestion was the best. A picnic with lots of people around. Hopefully, Justine would not be too disappointed.

I knocked on her door at eleven.

"Grady," Hayley greeted me. "Come in."

I stepped into the house and took off my hat. Justine entered the kitchen. She wore a bright yellow dress that made her golden hair shine. Her brown eyes lit with a smile when they connected with mine. She lifted a basket from the table. Then she strode over to me and placed a kiss on my cheek. My heart picked up pace.

"You mind if I leave my horse here?" I asked.

A frown flitted across her face before her smile chased it away. "Not at all."

I took the basket from her. Then I retrieved a blanket from behind my saddle. I offered my arm, and she looped her hand around it.

"I really intended to take you somewhere secluded," I admitted. "After last night's encounter with Caleb, it's safer to stay in public."

Justine nodded. "I trust you to know what's best. But I'm also concerned about this situation with Caleb. What is going on that makes you think it's not safe?"

We arrived at the plaza. I set the basket on the ground and shook out the blanket. Then I helped her sit down. She smiled sweetly and opened the basket as I took a seat.

"He threatened me. Being around me is not safe."

She handed me a sandwich and some iced tea.

I sighed. "Let's talk about something more pleasant, shall we?"

I took a bite of the sandwich to keep myself from scooting closer and pulling her into my arms. She asked me about the ranch. Then she asked me about my childhood home.

"Our farm is up past Chino Valley. Ellie Mae and I still own it. We have tenants that run the farm."

"Really? Do you want to move back?"

"No." I rubbed a hand on my pants. "I am planning a trip soon to see about selling it. I'm sure the tenants would be interested in buying it. They've asked about it a few times."

"And your sister agrees?"

"Yes. She's happy to live at the ranch with her husband and children. That's her home now."

"What about you, Grady? Is it home for you?" She sipped some iced tea.

"For now. I think Deacon will live there until the day he dies. Me? I would much rather live in town."

"Why don't you move? You have a good job. I wouldn't mind if you lived closer."

My pulse raced. I would love to be closer to my sweet Justine. Only the timing wasn't right.

I sighed. "I owe Deacon my life. He helped me more than I can ever explain. After my parents died and I moved to the ranch, Ellie Mae thought I might like to share a room with Deacon. I agreed because I had no choice."

I looked away and studied the pink bricks of the courthouse. I coughed. "It depressed me after losing my parents. My sister was so smitten with Sam that she didn't see it."

Justine shifted to sit next to me. She took my arm and ducked under it. Then she leaned into my side and looped her arms around my waist.

"I had nightmares for a long time. I saw..." My voice cracked. "My mother being shot in the head. Over and over.

The man in black. His gang."

I took a deep breath to chase away the darkness.

"Deacon saw it. He saw through my attempts to hide what was going on in my heart. Every time I screamed out from the nightmares, he woke and prayed over me."

I closed my eyes. I was a teenager again. In a strange home. Sharing a room with a kind stranger. I was awake and soaked from sweat despite a chilly room. Deacon laid a hand on my head. Words of comfort. Words of scripture.

Then I lashed out at him.

"He told me that the God of all creation knew the pain in my heart and that He loved me. He told me about Jesus. That this God that I knew about from church loved me so much He killed His own son to reconcile me."

I hugged Justine closer. I breathed in the scent of her soft hair. Lavender. Peaceful and sweet.

"After the fourth conversation like that, I finally asked him the question that my rage wanted answered, 'How can God love me so much if He took my parents away?' Do you know what he told me? My parents were not gone because God did something evil to me. Evil exists in the world and it touches our lives. Yet, God in His love sent me to Colter Ranch so I could experience the healing love of a family who cared for me as if I was their own."

Justine sniffed and dabbed at her eyes with her handkerchief.

"It was that night that I truly accepted what Jesus did for me and the love that God showed me."

I leaned back so I could look into her red-rimmed eyes.

"That was the night that God used Deacon Colter to save my life. Deacon is my best friend. He has his own heartache and carries a fair amount of pain wherever he goes. Yet, he cares deeply for every person who God puts in his path. He doesn't always say the right thing or act in a way that society expects. But no one has a bigger heart than Deacon."

Justine rubbed a hand on my back.

"So, for now, I live at the ranch because it is what Deacon needs. He took this new job because it's what I need. That's what we do. We sacrifice to help the other."

Justine said nothing. Instead, she leaned forward and placed a kiss on my cheek. Then she settled against my side again.

After several minutes, she finally said, "You are an incredible man, Grady Thatcher."

My heart warmed at her compliment. I wasn't sure why I bared my soul to her. Possibly because I hoped her heart felt as close to mine as mine did to hers.

CHAPTER 12

JUSTINE

My heart was no longer my own. After Grady laid his soul bare before me, he owned it. I was glad to let him have my heart. If I searched my entire life, I would not find a better man.

My sisters frequently discussed what a good and godly man looked like. Sometimes, I wondered if we made a fantastical image in our minds that could never be real.

Then I met Grady. He was better than what I dared to hope. He was so completely the opposite of my wretched father. Despite the deep wounds in his heart, he embraced a life of righteousness. More than just some moral code. No, his faith was genuine. Lived out in his friendship with Deacon. Lived out in his concern for my safety.

I sighed. "My father tried to barter us girls to his dark companions. Lilian suffered the most. I…"

Grady's arm tightened around me.

"I escaped with only a few bruises. I thank God we rescued Hayley before anything happened to her. As beautiful as she is…"

My voice broke and my eyes burned.

"I can't even think it."

After he kissed my forehead, he whispered, "You don't have to say more if you don't want to."

I straightened my back.

"Father is too gracious of a word to describe Galen Harper. He is an evil, wretched man. He hated us girls. Our only value, in his eyes, was as domestics. We were pawns to be married off to his despicable friends."

"Caleb Mason is such a man. His younger brother, Bart, is the kindest of the Mason brothers, though to say he is kind is untrue. He just never tried to take my virtue."

Grady stiffened.

"Not that he didn't lay a hand on me. He did. Especially when I refused his proposal."

"When did this happen?"

"A year ago. I thought he would do to me what Caleb did to Lilian. Instead, he left the area. After I moved here, I learned he works at the stockyards."

I took a deep breath before I continued. "When he came to the dry goods store a week ago, I feared what he might do. It surprised me when he apologized for being rough with me and said that he wished me well."

"Do you believe him?"

"I do. He differs from Victor and Caleb. The same darkness in them seems not so dark in Bart."

Grady rubbed his hand on my arm.

I pushed away. Then I flashed him a smile. "We should probably head back. Lilian will be worried."

I packed up the leftovers and placed them in the basket. He helped me up and then he carried our things.

"You know," I said as I nudged his arm. "We didn't eat our dessert. Perhaps you'll come in for pie?"

He laughed softly. "I would like that."

"I would apologize for our somber conversation, except I'm not sorry. I like that there are no secrets between us."

He held the door open for me.

"However, I would like to do something more fun on our next date."

He grinned as he set the basket down on the table. "I can help with that. Deacon and I would like you and your sisters to come for Sunday supper tomorrow."

I squealed and hugged him. "I would love it!"

Lilian stood and joined us in the kitchen. "I'm not attending church."

"Come on, Lilian," Hayley said. "It won't kill you to go one time. It's silly for us to come back here for you when we can leave from church."

Lilian frowned but said no more.

I started coffee on the stove to boil while Hayley dished up some pie. Grady smiled as I poured coffee for each of us.

When I sat next to him, he placed an arm on the back of my chair. I loved it. It made me feel protected and loved.

"This is good," he said between bites.

"Justine made it," Hayley said. "She is the best cook out of us."

Heat warmed my cheeks. "All three of us are fine cooks. I just occasionally like to bake something special."

"It's been forever since we had pie," Hayley confessed. "With Lilian and Justine working, we can afford nice things."

"Are you looking for a job, too?" Grady asked.

"Yes. I have an interview with a law firm in town on Monday. They are looking for a file and mail clerk. It sounded like it might be part time. But Lilian taught me the basics of office work, so I should do well."

I smiled. I was proud of Hayley for her desire to learn

new things. She embraced life, and I hoped she would never lose that.

When we finished our dessert, Grady lingered. My sisters went outside to bring in the laundry.

"I should really help them," I said as I stood.

"Alright. I ought to head back to the ranch anyway."

He pulled me into his arms. Then his brown-sugar eyes studied mine. "I enjoyed our day."

"Me too."

Then he lowered his lips to mine. He held me tight as his kiss deepened, and I kissed him back as my heart slipped further under his influence. I loved him. I knew it as he slowed his kiss.

When I saw the tender look in his eyes, I knew I owned his heart as much as he owned mine. It was far quicker than I ever expected.

I smiled as I slowed my breathing and released my hold on him.

"I'll see you tomorrow," I whispered.

"Looking forward to it, my sweet Justine."

With that, Grady left with my heart in his tender hands.

———

LILIAN

"I don't see why you put up such a fuss about church," Hayley challenged me as soon as we stepped outside to the clothesline.

I unpinned a dress from the line and stuffed the clothespins in my apron pocket. Then I shook out the dress and tossed it in the basket.

"You know why."

"It's one day. We aren't asking you to go every week. One day. With the promise of a date with Deacon. Surely that sweetens it."

"Is she still fuming?" Justine asked as she joined us.

"Of course."

I frowned. I did not want to attend church. Not for one day. Not for any reason. God abandoned me when I needed Him to protect me from Caleb. I couldn't forgive Him for that.

A small part of me knew if I went to church, I would lose the control that I so carefully crafted over the last year to protect my heart from further damage.

My entire life was about control. I controlled my fate by running away to Prescott. I took a job that let me feel in control and like I was catching evil men like Caleb and my father. Somehow, feeling like I controlled every aspect of my life helped me feel safe.

Going to church, singing those songs about surrendering my heart to God, I knew I would crumble. It required me to face things I avoided. So, no, I did not want to attend church, not even with the hope of a delightful afternoon with Deacon.

The next morning, I rose with my sisters and donned my best dress, despite my misgivings. My sisters smiled as I joined them for breakfast, but they said nothing.

I walked with them in silence to the church. When we arrived, Grady and Deacon greeted me warmly. I offered a tentative smile.

Grady introduced us to his sister, her husband, and children. They filled a pew on their own, along with Deacon's parents and sister. So we sat in the pew in front of them.

My heart squeezed tight as Grady sat on one end. Then

Justine, Hayley, me, and Deacon. Deacon blocked my way to the end of the pew. As the opening hymn started, I wrung my hands. I mumbled the words as Deacon held the hymnal for us. By the third song, I thought I might make it through the service.

Then the notes of the last hymn filled my ears. Hayley bellowed the words, "I surrender all."

A lump formed in my throat. My breathing shallowed. I frowned and glanced around frantically.

"Let me out," I whispered to Deacon.

When he saw my eyes, he hastened to the aisle.

I ran outside and down the stairs. The need to flee overwhelmed. I must hide. I must escape.

Strong arms grabbed me from behind. I screamed. A hand clamped over my mouth as the voice from my nightmares whispered in my ear.

"Hello my Harper harlot."

Caleb.

My eyes went wide. I squirmed and fought against him. He would not abuse me again. I reached for the pistol in my dress pocket.

CHAPTER 13

DEACON

"All three of them will attend church, right?" I asked Grady for the third time.

"Relax, Deacon. Lilian will be there. Even if she doesn't normally go, Justine promised she would be there."

I took a deep breath as I headed to the barn to saddle Sergeant. My heart broke a little when Grady told me that Lilian didn't like church. Last night, he said that her sister had said she stopped going after her relationship with Caleb. The shadow that fell across his face confirmed my suspicion that Caleb had hurt Lilian deeply.

From the moment he told me that, I prayed for her. Throughout the night and the morning. I prayed she would learn to deal with whatever drove her away from church.

When we arrived at church, I saw the fear in her eyes immediately. I was pretty sure she wanted to sit at the end of the row, but I hoped if I sat there, it might bring her comfort. Once the fourth song started, she nudged me and asked me to let her out.

The pain in her tear-filled eyes caused my heart to ache. I stepped into the aisle as I prayed for her heart. I glanced at

Mama. She nodded, so I followed Lilian out of the church.

Before I opened the door, I heard her scream. I flung the church doors open.

Caleb Mason held her tight in his grip. Her eyes were full of terror.

"Grady!" I called for him as I drew my pistol.

Grady, Boone, Sam, and Perry Quinn followed me out the door. The sheriff was in the service and joined us outside.

"Let her go!" I hollered as I rushed down the stairs.

I froze when Caleb drew a knife and pressed it against her neck.

"Stop right there or I end her."

The darkness in his expression halted me. I couldn't get a clean shot without fear of hitting Lil.

The sheriff caught my eye. He motioned that he and Perry were going to circle around behind Caleb. Grady must have noticed their signal, because he started talking.

"Caleb, let her go. Isn't it me you really want?"

My heart stopped beating for a second. I wouldn't let Grady give himself up.

Caleb laughed. "I want her more right now than I want you. I know where to find you, Thatcher. When my boss says it's your time, you won't see me coming."

Lilian stopped struggling. I sent another prayer heavenward to protect her. I willed her to keep fighting as Caleb shuffled closer to his horse.

"Let her go!" I demanded again.

I saw something come over her. She turned to face him, and my stomach churned.

"I'll give you what you want, Caleb."

My jaw twitched as she placed one hand on his cheek. She did not want any such thing. His eyes went wide as his attention turned to her. I took a few steps closer while she distracted him.

Then I heard a pistol fire. Caleb stumbled backwards, away from Lilian. Her entire body shook as the gun slipped from her fingers. I ran to her before she collapsed.

The rage in Caleb's eyes was unmistakable as he hobbled toward his horse, dragging his bloodied foot behind him.

I pulled Lilian into my arms, and she buried her head against my chest.

"Did I kill him?"

Caleb mounted his horse. The sheriff and Perry mounted theirs and followed him as he rode out of town.

"No, though he'll limp for some time."

Justine and Hayley swarmed her. I released Lilian to their care as my hands shook.

"Did that just happen?" Boone asked.

"Did Lilian just shoot Caleb Mason?" Grady asked.

I nodded numbly.

"I'll let the congregation know the danger is over," Boone said. Then he ducked inside the church.

I guided the Harper sisters over to our wagon and suggested they sit down. Lilian's skin looked gray. Her eyes looked hollow. Her body still shook.

"He was going to... Again," she whispered to her sisters.

"You did good, Lilian. That's why we bought the gun for you," Justine said.

"He's never going to hurt you again. Not with all these witnesses," Hayley reassured her.

Grady and I walked away from the wagon and searched the area for signs of the rest of the Mason Gang. Seemed like he acted alone that morning.

The music for the final hymn faded. Then the parishioners exited the building. My family offered their support.

When I brought Lilian some water, she stared past me but took it.

Then we headed home. Ellie Mae drove the wagon with all the women and children, including the Harper sisters, riding in the back. Papa and Sam rode ahead while Grady and I flanked the wagon. I scanned the area as we went.

My heart broke over the trauma Lilian had suffered. I hoped she wouldn't push me away out of fear. I loved her. The moment Caleb held the knife to her throat, I realized I would have killed him if it meant protecting her.

That thought disturbed me. I was supposed to save lives, not take them.

For the first time, I realized my new job would require some tough decisions. If Grady and I found the Mason Gang's hideout, I believed they would put up a fight. I might face the decision to take someone's life in order to save another's.

Grady offered to take care of my horse when we arrived home. "See to Lilian."

When I helped her down from the wagon, she clutched me as if I could somehow pass strength to her.

"Would you like to take a walk?" I asked softly.

She nodded.

Justine gave me a half smile, which I took to mean her sisters thought my suggestion was a good idea.

As we walked toward the lake, I held Lilian close to my side. I took her to the dock and helped her sit there. We both dangled our feet over the edge.

"I shot him," she whispered.

"In the foot."

She snorted. "I suppose that was effective."

"The sheriff and Perry Quinn took off after him. He won't get far. He's gonna pay for this, Lil."

She went limp against me. Then she hid her face in her hands and sobbed. I rubbed my hand on her arm and let her cry.

At length, I saw Grady wave from the porch. It was suppertime.

"Are you hungry? Let's eat with the family. Or I could bring you a plate and we can sit out here."

"Some first impression I've made on your family."

"I think you'll find my family to be very understanding."

I stood and offered her my hand. She took it. Once she stood, she took a deep breath. Then she squared her shoulders and let it out slowly.

"Alright. Let's see how true that is."

Then she looped her hand in the crook of my arm as I led her to the house.

The conversation continued around us as we sat at the table. My family made her feel welcome, and she relaxed as the meal wound down.

———

GRADY

As soon as supper finished, I asked Justine to stroll around the lake. The information she provided during our picnic date was helpful, and after all Lilian endured that morning, I knew Deacon would not ply her with questions. It would have been cruel.

"Tell me more about your childhood home," I said as I laced my fingers with hers.

She sighed. "Our father was always involved in a scheme. As children, we didn't understand that he was an outlaw. As we grew up, Shane and Lilian learned our father was not like other fathers."

Justine stared at the lake. Then she straightened her back and continued.

"Unsavory men came by the house. As Shane grew older, he tried to protect us from those men. He kept them out in the barn. Eventually, he converted the tack room into a hangout for the men. That kept them away from the house."

"Shane devised a system. He hung a red bandanna on one of the hat hooks by the door. That meant to stay in the house and yard. Not to come to the barn. It wasn't safe. Be careful washing the laundry."

"A blue bandanna on the hat hook meant we were free to roam anywhere on the property."

My heart ached. How horrible to feel unsafe at home.

"Sometimes the men stayed for weeks or months on end. Papa made us do their laundry and cook extra food for the men. Only he didn't give us more money to buy food or help to butcher chickens, pigs, or cattle for meat. He left us to figure out how to stretch our meager food supplies to feed so many people."

"Mama was no help. She spent most days sick in bed. As soon as Lilian and I were old enough to manage the house, we rarely saw her outside of mealtimes."

I stopped when I found a pleasant spot to sit, as I sensed her story was far from over.

"When Mama passed on a few years before we left, Papa started taking his rage out on Lilian or me. Shane learned a long time ago not to interfere, lest he suffer under Papa's brutal hand."

"I never understood why he didn't touch Hayley, Flynn, or Ike. A part of me was jealous, wondering what Lilian and

I did to deserve such harsh treatment. A part of me was relieved that he spared them."

She drew her knees close to her chest and wrapped her arms around them.

"When Hayley and I boarded a stagecoach to Prescott, that was the best day of my life. I hope my younger brothers fare better than we did."

I waited for several minutes before I asked, "The Masons. Were they among the rough men that stayed on the ranch?"

She nodded. "Victor and Caleb came by. After a few years, Caleb was determined to have Lilian. Once he started," she coughed, "courting, for lack of a better word, Bart came around. I never sensed he was as deeply involved as his brothers."

"What about Victor?"

"He is pure evil. His heart is as black as the clothes he wears."

I straightened. "He wears all black?"

"Yes."

"Did Lilian ever meet him?"

Justine cocked her head to the side. "Now that you mention it, I don't think so. It was an accident that I did. Bart had taken me to the barn one night to kiss me." When she shuddered, I wondered if he had more sinister intentions. "Victor caught us and scolded Bart. Told him not to bring us girls to the barn. That Galen would be angry."

She snorted. "I doubted Papa would be angry. Especially since he kept pushing Lilian and I to marry the two younger Mason brothers."

She sighed heavily. "Why are all our conversations so heavy, Grady? Can't we talk about the future? Dream of a different life from one so full of sorrows."

"You're right," I said as I vowed to show her the sketch of the man in black soon.

"So, how many children do you want?" I winked at her.

She laughed. "I wasn't aware that I got to choose."

"Humor me."

"I don't know that I've ever thought about it. I'm more concerned with finding a decent, God-fearing man who will treat me like a princess."

I stood to my feet and helped her up. Then I swept her into my arms. "A princess, you say?"

She giggled. "At the very least, like I am special."

"No, no. I heard princess." I stooped down and lifted her into my arms.

"Grady, what are you doing? You don't have to carry me."

I grinned as I set her feet down after a few steps. "Good. I couldn't carry you back to the house."

"You could kiss me, if you'd like."

"Now, I can agree with that."

CHAPTER 14

LILIAN

By midafternoon, I was exhausted. I sat on the couch next to Deacon in the parlor of his brother's house. My eyes grew droopy, and I must have fallen asleep because Deacon tapped my arm.

He whispered in my ear, "Let me take you home."

I nodded.

When he stood, so did Grady and my sisters.

Grady smiled. "Harper Sisters, would you care to ride in the wagon or on a horse?"

"Horse." Justine said, and Hayley echoed her.

They ran ahead with Grady toward the barn. I walked slowly next to Deacon.

"Thank you for everything," I said. "Your family is really wonderful."

"I'm glad they made you feel welcome."

"Deacon?"

"Hmm?"

"Can I ride with you?"

A grin lit his face. "Absolutely."

"I apologize in advance if I fall asleep again."

He turned to face me. "You've been through a lot today. It's understandable."

He rubbed his thumb on my cheek and smirked.

I smiled. "What's so funny?"

"I... I like," he took his finger and pointed to the freckle by my left eye, "this. It makes me smile."

Heat warmed my face.

As my sisters saddled the horses Grady suggested for them, I waited in the barn. Grady and Deacon saddled their own.

Then Deacon let me mount his horse before he slid into place behind me. When he took the reins, his arms came around me. Leaning back against him, I felt safe in his arms. He rested one arm around my waist.

"Wouldn't want you to slip if you doze off." His breath was warm on my cheek.

I rested my arms over the one that held me tight.

"Rest easy, Lil. I've got you."

Before I knew it, Deacon pulled his horse up in front of my house. He dismounted and helped me down.

"What's this?" Justine said. She pulled a paper off the front door and held it out.

Grady read it aloud. "Caleb is in custody. Will talk tomorrow. PQ."

"Oh, from Perry," I said.

"That's good news," Hayley said. "We can all stop worrying now."

"Lil." Deacon stopped me before I entered the house. "Will you be alright?"

As he settled his hands on my waist, his deep brown eyes searched mine. When tears burned my eyes, I nodded and looked away. He placed a soft kiss on my forehead and released me.

"See you in the morning."

As soon as Deacon and Grady left, I changed into my nightgown and went to bed, despite the early hour.

The next morning, I woke refreshed. I slept better than I had in weeks.

"Good luck with your interview," I said to Hayley as I finished my breakfast. I checked my hair one more time before I opened the door.

Deacon stood leaning against the post of the porch. When he saw me, he smiled.

"Morning, Lil."

My heart fluttered at the sight of him. "Morning."

He pushed away from the post and offered me his arm. "You look lovely today."

Heat warmed my face. "Thank you."

Neither of us said anything else on the walk to the office. I appreciated he continued to walk me to work, even though Caleb was behind bars.

Perry Quinn waited for us in the office. As soon as we entered, he called the four of us into his office.

"Xavier, dig into Bart Mason's background. See if he's been working with Caleb and the Mason Gang."

Grady cleared his throat. "I have a lead on the identity of the man in black."

"Good, chase that down. Let us know what you find. Deacon, I want you to take Lilian over to the sheriff to file an official report about what happened yesterday and anything else that Lilian cares to share about Caleb."

I felt the blood drain from my face. My hands shook.

"Lilian." Perry softened his tone. "You can do this. You did nothing wrong. Right now, there's not enough evidence to link Caleb to the rustling, so we need you to help us file strong enough charges to keep him behind bars until we can finish our investigation."

I nodded numbly.

"Can the sheriff interview me at my home?" I asked.

"Yes," Deacon said. "I'll drop you off and go fetch him."

Within a half hour, the sheriff sat across from me at my kitchen table. Deacon rested his arm on the back of my chair as I relayed what had happened on Sunday.

"Has Caleb ever done anything to harm you?" the sheriff asked.

I frowned as rage burned within me. "He forced himself on me. Several times when I lived at my family's ranch."

Deacon sucked in a sharp breath. I glanced at him. His jaw twitched, and his eyes darkened.

"Whenever I refused, he would rough me up first. I eventually learned to just let him..." My voice broke, then I breathed deeply. "I learned to let him do what he wanted."

I looked at the corner of the room as I weighed the cost of saying more. Surely, Deacon would want nothing to do with me. Not after that. If I confessed the worst of it, he would never want me.

"Is there something else, Miss Harper?" the sheriff asked.

Tears rolled down my cheeks. I locked my eyes on the sheriff. "Isn't that enough?"

He smiled sympathetically as he slid a piece of paper and pencil across the table. "I will need dates. Witnesses. Any further details you can provide will strengthen the case."

I swiped at the tears on my cheeks and took the pencil. Then I spent the next several minutes documenting each date. I knew them by heart.

———

DEACON

As Lilian's list of abuse grew longer and longer, I straightened my back and clamped my jaw tight. Caleb Mason was the worst kind of man.

Fourteen. Fourteen times that man hurt my Lil.

As I felt my control slipping away, I told Lilian I would wait for her outside. I didn't want to frighten her.

When I stepped onto her porch, I tried to regain control. I rubbed my thumb against my index finger. I counted the number of boards on her porch, then I categorized the boards with knots versus the ones without.

Lord, please help me.

Nothing more specific formed in my mind.

I closed my eyes and took a deep breath, like when I wanted to sing loudly. Then I let it out slowly. I did that several times before I felt controlled again.

A few minutes later, Lilian and the sheriff exited her house. She seemed fine. The sheriff thanked her for her help.

When I offered her my arm, she took it. As we walked, I didn't realize I was rubbing my thumb on my finger again.

"Are you alright?" she asked.

I glanced down and willed myself to stop the nervous habit.

"Fine."

We walked for a block before I asked her the same.

She sighed. "I just hope the sheriff does something about Caleb."

I nodded.

As soon as we returned to the office, I was immediately aware of the uneven space between the chairs in the lobby. I set about fixing it.

"Deacon, what are you doing?" Lilian asked.

I could not explain it as I repositioned all the chairs to be two inches apart instead of the odd spacing before.

As she stood next to me, she placed a hand on my arm. I stilled for a moment.

"The chairs are off."

I wasn't sure when she left my side and returned to her desk. After I fixed the chairs, I moved on to the coffee mugs. I positioned each of them so the handle pointed the same direction. When I eyed her desk, she stood.

"Don't even think about it. What has gotten into you?"

I paced the room. Thankfully, we were the only two people in the office. At least my boss didn't witness my odd behavior.

"Deacon, sit."

After I sat in one chair across from her desk, I stood and lined them up perfectly before I sat in one again.

"What is going on?"

I sighed. "I'm sorry."

My leg bobbed up and down.

Lilian moved to sit in the chair next to me. She took my hand in hers. Then she waited.

I closed my eyes. "I'm sorry. When I get upset, I must fix things. Like... Like the brand wall. Only worse. It makes little sense."

When I opened my eyes, hers gleamed with compassion instead of judgement.

"When I'm upset, disorder bothers me more. I have to fix them. I don't know how else to say it."

"I think I understand," she whispered. "When I feel out of control, I want to control something, anything. Controlling something makes me feel safe."

"I guess it's kinda like that, only worse. I can't stop myself from doing it."

Completely embarrassed by my strange behavior, I looked away.

"Thank you."

My head swiveled to her, and I raised an eyebrow.

"I'm touched that you care so much about me that what I went through bothers you so deeply."

I cleared my throat. Then I placed a hand on her cheek. "I'm so sorry, Lil, that no one protected you."

A few tears leaked from her eyes. She squeezed my hand before she sat behind her desk and dabbed her eyes dry.

Then she smiled at me. "Thank you again, Deacon."

I walked into the other room, and I sat at my desk. Then I stared at the wall until the end of the day.

Then I walked Lilian home before I rode to the ranch alone, since Grady did not return to the office.

I wanted to ask my mama for some advice, but that would betray Lilian, so I kept it to myself. As soon as supper was over, I retired to my room and I prayed.

CHAPTER 15

GRADY

After Perry gave us our assignments for the day, I grabbed the sketch book and flipped to the picture of the man in black. I folded it and stuffed it in my pocket. Then I headed over to the dry goods store.

When I entered, Justine greeted me.

"Morning, beautiful." I flashed her my most charming grin.

"Slow day at the office?"

"Can't a fella decide to stop by and see his girl?"

She laughed. "So I'm your girl now?"

"I recall treating you like a princess yesterday."

She smiled. "What really brings you here?"

"If truth be told, I need a favor."

I unfolded the paper and smoothed it out. Then I handed it to her. "Have you ever seen this man?"

She held the paper and studied it for merely a few seconds. Then she thrust it back at me as she frowned.

"It's Victor Mason."

As I folded the paper, my hands shook. I put it back in my pocket. At last, I knew the name of my parents' murderer.

"Is he the man in black?"

I nodded grimly.

Justine reached for my hand and squeezed. "I'm so sorry, Grady."

"I'm not. After six long years, I finally have a name. I can work with a name."

"Stop by after work. Have supper with us."

"Thank you, but I think Lilian is going to want a quiet evening. She's meeting with the sheriff today to give her statement."

"Come by anyway. We can walk together before you head home."

I leaned over the counter and kissed her cheek. "Thanks, my thoughtful Justine. I may take you up on the offer."

She wished me well before I left the store.

I showed the picture at the different liveries in town. When I showed it to Thomas Anderson, he recognized Victor right away.

"Yeah, he usually boards his horse here when he comes to town. His brother, Caleb, does too."

"When did you last see him?"

Thomas rubbed a hand on his chin. "He was here early last week. Or maybe the weekend before."

My heart raced. That coincided with the day he showed up at the livestock office. He could have delivered the Thompson's stolen cattle. I had no proof. Yet.

"Did he say anything? Do you know if he drove some livestock into town?"

Thomas took a seat on his stool by the workbench and rubbed his knee. "He said nothing. Usually doesn't. But Caleb mentioned a big sale that they were a part of. Something about thirty or forty head of cattle they just sold to the stockyards."

"Do you know when they sold it?"

"Not sure. Sometime in January or early February. I don't recall the exact date when they were here last."

I shook Thomas's hand and thanked him for the information.

Then I headed over to the stockyards. I went to see Derek Gardner.

"Xavier just left," Derek said when I entered his office.

"Yeah, I heard new information since I last saw him." I handed Derek the sketch. "Do you know this man?"

"Can't say I know his name. He looks awful familiar, though. May have been a foreman or cowboy with a recent crew. You might show his picture around to see if anyone else has seen him."

"Thanks for your time."

I discreetly showed the picture around, as I didn't want Bart to get wind of it. A few other staff members thought he looked familiar, but none of them knew his name.

My stomach growled. I missed lunch, so I went to the café and ordered a sandwich. As I sat there, the waves of emotion threatened to push forward. I stuffed it down in order to finish my investigation.

After dark, I headed over to the Palace. I showed the sketch to the bartender. He recognized Victor immediately.

"Yeah. Comes in every couple of months. Not very popular with the girls. He treats them rough."

I schooled my features. Seemed that all the Mason men treated women poorly.

"He in town now?" I asked.

"Not that I know."

Like last time, I ordered a beer and water. As I slowly sipped it, the saloon came alive. The piano player pounded out an upbeat tune on the tinny sounding instrument. Saloon girls flirted with patrons. Men played cards and smoked cigars.

I pulled my hat lower over my face to shade my eyes. Then I turned around and faced the main part of the saloon. While I scanned the crowd, I leaned back against the bar and sipped my beer. I noticed Amos Thompson sat at a table with a group of men. None of them resembled any of the Mason brothers.

A saloon girl sauntered up to me and draped herself over my chest. I started to push her away when she said something that caught my attention.

"I heard you're asking about Victor Mason."

I pretended to be interested so we could carry on the conversation without drawing suspicion.

"Last week, he was bragging to Josie about pulling one over on the stockyards. Said he had himself a rock-solid con going on."

To keep the ruse going, I flashed her a charming grin.

"You have a right fine smile," she said before she continued. "He's memorized a dozen brands for the county that would be easy to burn over. Thompson's. Wendel Franks. Georgie Larson. Among others."

"When will he be back?"

"A couple of weeks. Early March. He fancies Josie."

I took a few bills and handed them to her.

"You sure you don't want some entertainment?"

"Move along now."

She took the bills and rolled them up. Then she stuffed them in her bodice before she sashayed away.

I downed the last of my beer and ordered another when I remembered Justine had offered for me to stop by.

Though I wouldn't mind seeing her beautiful face, I was

too much trouble for her. If the Mason Gang intended to harm me, just being around me could get her killed.

I faced the bar again. I should stop seeing her until it was safe.

My head floated as I ordered a third drink. After six long years, I finally had solid information about the man who had murdered my parents. I knew his name, when he would be in town again, and some ranchers he targeted. Most were between Prescott and Ash Fork.

As I stood, dizziness washed over me, and I steadied myself. I left the saloon and headed toward Justine's house. Worried for her safety, I sat on a neighbor's porch and watched her home. Light came from a window. When a woman's silhouette appeared, I quickly ducked down out of sight.

A deep breath left my lungs. I loved her. I wanted to make our relationship official. Instead, I knew I must break it off. It was the best thing for her.

As the noise of the saloons faded, I curled up and fell asleep.

The next morning, I woke to a broom landing hard on my head.

"Get out of here, you vagrant!" A woman screamed hysterically as she beat me with the broom.

I stood and headed toward the livestock office to report what I had learned the night before.

Deacon and Lilian were already at the office.

"Where have you been?" Deacon asked as soon as he saw me.

"Saloon. Got info on the man in black. He is none other than Victor Mason."

Lilian gasped.

After I pulled Deacon into Perry's office, I relayed what I

knew. He said he'd tell Perry and Xavier. Then he sent me home to clean up.

As I entered the lobby again, Lilian confronted me.

"Justine waited for you until nine last night."

"Yeah, well," I said with an edge to my voice, "I didn't promise her anything."

When Lilian said something else, I interrupted her.

"You tell Justine that she best forget about me."

The shock on Lilian's face said everything. My heart tore in two. The very last thing I wanted was to leave my sweet Justine, but I reminded myself it was for her own good.

———

JUSTINE

When Lilian came home on Tuesday and told me that Grady said I should forget him, a knife sliced deep into my heart. I did not understand what I had done to drive him away. Two days ago, he asked me about children and the things couples discuss when they become serious.

I watched for him every day for the rest of the week. He never came by the shop or my home.

When Sunday came, I planned to confront him at church. Only he didn't give me the opportunity. He sat in his sister's pew with one of his nephews on each side.

Deacon sat next to Lilian. Then Hayley. Then me. The place where Grady belonged remained empty.

I glanced back at him a few times. Each time, his gaze darted away.

My heart broke as my sisters, and I walked home from church.

"What happened?" Hayley asked.

"I don't know."

After we ate, I hid in my room. My mind whirled with a thousand thoughts.

Did Grady only get close to me to get information about the Mason Gang? So many of our conversations centered on my past, or Lilian's, and the Masons. Perhaps Grady did not really have feelings for me, after all.

As the days rolled into weeks, my heart decided that Grady never cared for me. He only used me to get information about the men who murdered his parents. He didn't love me.

If only I could stop loving him.

CHAPTER 16

DEACON

Two weeks later, they released Caleb Mason. We failed to provide the evidence against him for rustling. The district attorney decided not to press charges on behalf of Lilian for crimes from over a year ago, with no one to corroborate her version of the events. It was her word against his.

Lilian stayed home from work for a few days.

On the morning of March third, I showed up on her doorstep to walk her to work again. She beamed as she exited her home.

"Morning," she greeted me. "I enjoy starting the day walk-ing with you."

I smiled. "Me too."

I was relieved that she seemed in better spirits than I expected. Perhaps the time off helped.

"Deacon!"

We were almost at the office when someone called my name. I turned to see Derek Gardner running towards me.

"We need your help at the stockyards right away."

"What's going on?"

"We've got a group of sick cattle I think you should

look at in your official role with the livestock inspection office."

"Alright. Should I have Lilian send Grady over?"

He nodded.

"Better send Perry, too," I told Lilian.

She walked the last few blocks on her own as I followed Derek to the stockyards.

"Think it might be foot and mouth," Derek said.

My stomach plummeted. "Do you have them in isolation?"

"Yes, but they arrived on the train."

"Do you know what train? When did they come in? Where are they from?"

Derek rubbed a hand over his face. "They came in yester-day afternoon from Georgie Larson's ranch up near Ash Fork, according to the paperwork."

I followed Derek inside. I grabbed a pair of overalls and rubber gloves that were kept at the stockyards' vet office for just such a reason. Then I met Derek inside.

As soon as I saw the cattle, I knew Derek was right. Oozing sores and ulcers covered the mouths of several head. It was foot and mouth. From the looks of it, the stockyards probably received the cattle with obvious signs of the disease. They were much further along than the six-day incubation period. They should have refused them and called us immediately, not the next day.

Perry, Grady, and Lilian arrived a few minutes later.

"Someone needs to visit Georgie Larson's ranch right now," I said.

"I'll go," Grady volunteered.

Perry agreed. "Lilian, go contact the Central Arizona Railway. Tell Bullock to trace all the livestock from that car. They also must pull it from service immediately and sanitize it with coal tar."

"Anything else before I head over there?"

"Telegraph to Ash Fork. Find out if they mixed other cattle in with Larson's. If so, get the origination."

Lilian left.

"Have they isolated these?" Perry asked.

"Yes," Derek answered. "We typically quarantine them for a few days before we mix them with the herd."

"And you use separate shovels, pitchforks, all tools, and gear?"

Derek frowned. "Well, no."

I shook my head. "This is highly contagious and can spread from direct contact with an infected animal, feces, water, etc. You understand?"

"We'll sanitize everything and start using separate tools," Derek agreed.

"I'm going to examine all the other livestock here," I said. "Nothing gets shipped out until we've assessed the impact. Likely won't be shipping anything out for six days or more."

"But—"

"No exceptions, Gardner," Perry said. "You also won't be receiving any new livestock at this location. Set up some temporary corrals away from here for new arrivals. We must segregate new livestock until we know the full extent of the outbreak."

"Even then, we'll want to start some strict sanitation protocols," I added. "Every person must wear overalls, rubber gloves, and rubber boots. They must launder overalls after each use. We must thoroughly sanitize gloves and boots from corral to corral."

"Anything that touches the livestock must be sanitized," Perry said.

"Our goal is to prevent the spread by being cautious. We don't want to risk contaminating healthy cattle by introducing the virus from our clothing and equipment."

Perry walked with Derek to his office to outline more procedures.

I spent the rest of the day examining the newest arrivals at the stockyards. There was nothing to be done but to destroy roughly one hundred head from various ranches.

Derek assigned Bart Mason to help catalog the animals destined for death. He recorded the number of cattle and the originating ranch.

After the sun set, Lilian stopped by.

"I left some supper for you in the vet's office."

I smiled as I finished examining the last steer in the corral. Then I opened the gate and stepped through.

"Give me a minute to clean up."

"I'll wait for you in the office."

I hurried to the sink to sanitize my rubber gloves and rubber boots. Then I discarded my overalls in the laundry basket before I scrubbed my hands and arms with coal tar soap.

Once I joined Lilian in the office, the smell of food hit my nostrils and my stomach growled. I sat at the desk while she sat on a stool.

"When are you going home?" she asked.

"Not until we have this under control."

"Do you want me to send word to the ranch? Do you want a change of clothes?"

I swallowed a bite of the stew she made. "Yes, that would be nice."

She filled me in on the other efforts while I ate. When I finished the meal, I stood. She did as well. Then she stepped close and stood on her tiptoes and kissed me. On the lips.

I wrapped my arms around her and gave her a sound kiss back. When I released her, rosy splotches appeared on her cheeks.

"Thanks for taking care of me," I said as I held the door open for her.

When she took the dishes with her and waved goodbye, my heart danced.

The next day, I oversaw the slaughter and burial. We dug a massive pit over six feet deep, where we dumped the carcasses of the diseased animals. Then we covered the bodies with quicklime before a few men buried them with dirt. It took three days.

I stayed at the stockyards for another week to oversee the sanitation. Each evening, Lilian brought me a meal, and I sat and listened to her updates while I scarfed down the food. I slept on the couch in my old office. Each morning, I left for a quick breakfast before I started the day.

It was nine days before I returned home for one night's sleep, only to turn around the next morning and ride back to the stockyards to keep close watch on all the incoming cattle.

By the fourteenth day, I was confident we had eradicated the outbreak at the stockyards. I hoped Grady fared well in the north.

CHAPTER 17

GRADY

The day of the outbreak, I had no time to run home. Sunbeam and I boarded the train and headed north to Meath, which was the train stop where the infected cattle came from.

It frustrated me to be gone from Prescott in early March, as that was when Victor was due in town.

But part of my job was to handle situations like disease outbreaks. That was why the livestock inspection office hired veterinarians, after all.

Once I arrived in Meath, I retrieved Sunbeam. Then I rode east to Georgie Larson's ranch. The landscape was flat, open prairie land with a few deep washes.

After about an hour, I arrived at Larson's Ranch. No one appeared in the barn and no cattle were corralled. After I tied Sunbeam to the hitching post, I knocked on the door.

A middle-aged, dark-haired woman greeted me. "Good afternoon."

"My name is Grady Thatcher. I believe you know my co-worker, Deacon Colter?"

"Yes, what is this about?" she asked cautiously. She

opened the door only a crack.

"I'm with the livestock inspection office. Is Georgie here?"

She hesitated. "He's out with the herd."

I smiled, hoping to set her at ease. "Mrs. Larson, could I trouble you for some water? I've traveled all the way from Prescott this morning."

"You said you know the Colters?"

I nodded.

"I suppose it'd be alright if you came in. My name is Emmy."

She offered me a seat at the table. Then she poured me a glass of water and sat across from me.

"What is your business?"

"I'd prefer to discuss it with Georgie, if I might?"

"He's not due back until suppertime. If you want to ride northeast, you'll probably find him and the herd approximately thirty minutes away."

"Thank you kindly, Emmy."

I finished the water and rode out. As Sunbeam plodded over the desolate landscape, I wondered why Georgie Larson would take his sickly herd out to pasture. With the contagious nature of foot and mouth disease, surely he would have quarantined the sick animals near his homestead so he could control the outbreak.

When I saw the herd in the distance, I waved. A man rode toward me.

"Hello, there!" I kept my voice friendly and light as he approached, riding a pinto gelding. Once he was within earshot, I introduced myself and mentioned my connection to the Colters.

"Georgie Larson." The man gave his name curtly. "What brings you here?"

"I'm with the livestock inspection office. There's an outbreak of foot and mouth at the stockyards in Prescott. The paperwork showed the cattle came in with your brand."

He frowned and rested his hand on the handle of his holstered pistol. "I have shipped no cattle southward in six months or more."

I bit back my surprise. "Well, the paperwork we received said the cattle came in from Larson Ranch. Brand matched your registered mark."

"Did the bill of sale show the chain of custody?"

"Yes, it listed your ranch as the origination."

"How old were these cattle?"

Crud. I had not verified the age of the animals. I'd have to wire Perry for the answer.

"You said you have shipped nothing south?"

He nodded.

"Seen any signs of disease among your herd or other livestock?"

"No, sir."

"Mind if I inspect your herd?"

He shifted in his saddle. "Is that really necessary?"

"I mean no offense, Georgie. Part of my job is to inspect brands and the overall health of livestock. I've got an odd mystery to solve here, and it sure would help me if I can rule out anything amiss with your herd."

"Come on." He motioned for me to follow him back to the herd.

Once we stopped, I dismounted and began inspecting the cattle. I retrieved my notebook from my saddlebags, then I asked Georgie about the brand. He confirmed the brand I saw on the first steer was indeed the correct brand. I compared it to my previous sketch from the registered brands wall. It matched.

After several hours, I found no evidence of any brand burning or disease among his herd.

"This is your entire herd?"

"Yes. Except for the bull we corral at the ranch."

"And you have noticed none missing or any sickness? Any other livestock mixed in with your herd?"

"Nothing of the sort."

I rubbed a hand over my chin. None of it made any sense. The paperwork clearly showed the infected cattle came from Larson's ranch. Yet everything was in perfect order.

"I'm gonna head back to the ranch. Would you care to join us for supper?" he asked.

I accepted the offered meal and a spot in the barn to sleep for the night.

The next morning after breakfast, I got a copy of Georgie's signature and his foreman's for my records so I could compare them to the paperwork back in Prescott. Then I headed back to Meath.

I wired Perry Quinn for further instructions. While I waited for a response, I headed to the small saloon. I struck up a conversation with the bartender, who was annoyed when I only ordered a sarsaparilla.

"You hear of any rustling around here?" I asked.

The bartender looked up for a moment. "Not recently. Around three months ago, Matt Clark lost about thirty head in a raid by some bandits."

"What about sick animals? Cattle, sheep, horses?"

"Ain't heard nothing about that."

An hour later, I checked in with the telegrapher. He had a response for me. "Investigate other ranches in the area."

I sighed. I hoped to get back in time for whatever Victor Mason was plotting.

Instead, I headed out to Matt Clark's ranch. Learned nothing more from him than I had from the bartender in Meath.

I spent the next three weeks visiting most of the ranches between Ash Fork, Seligman, and Prescott. Not a single animal had any signs of disease.

Finally, in the middle of April, Perry called me back home. When the train arrived in Prescott, I headed straight to the office to meet with Perry, Deacon, Xavier, and Lilian.

"You look rough," Lilian greeted me.

I nodded.

"Smell it too," Deacon teased. That earned him a half-smile from me.

I was exhausted and just wanted to provide my report and go home.

"Clark, Jackson, and Ackers all reported missing cattle around the early part of January," I said. "No one else had missing cattle. No diseased or sick livestock of any kind. I must have visited thirty ranches or more."

Deacon told me about the destruction of cattle at the stockyards.

"What makes little sense to me," he said, "was that the paperwork shows Larson's ranch as the origin of the cattle."

"Did you verify the brand?" I asked.

"I thought I did. To be honest, I don't think I studied the brands too closely," he admitted. "I was trying to contain the outbreak."

"You got a copy of the paperwork?"

Lilian handed it to me. I pulled out my notes and went back to Georgie's signature and his foreman's. I held it up against the seller's signature. It did not match.

"This is a forgery," I said. Then I handed my notebook and the paperwork to Perry.

Perry studied it for a moment. Then he nodded.

"Let's call it a day. Tomorrow we'll go through our records to verify the signatures of everything that came through the stockyards since the end of February. Good work, Grady."

I shuffled out of the office and headed to the bathhouse at the Palace. I got a shave, cut, and a much needed bath. Then I put on clean clothes, which Deacon brought to the office for me, and I headed home.

A pang of guilt settled in my stomach. I missed Justine and wanted to see her. Instead, I held firm to my resolve that it wasn't safe for her to be around me. Not until I tracked down Victor Mason.

CHAPTER 18

JUSTINE

My twentieth birthday arrived. It was on a Saturday that year. I wished I was excited, but all I could think about was Grady. I had not seen him for two months. He had not been at church, either. Lilian told me he traveled all over the northern part of the territory for his job.

"Grady's back in town," she said as the three of us laundered our clothes.

"How is he?" I tried to keep the concern from my voice.

"He didn't come into the office yesterday. I don't blame him. He worked his tail off the last few weeks on his own."

I ran a dress through the wringer to squeeze all the excess water from the garment before Hayley pinned it to the line.

My heart missed him. My mind tried to convince me he never loved me and that his rejection of me was not truly for my good. Lilian and I had the same conversation repeatedly. She agreed with Grady that it was too dangerous for him to be around me. I didn't believe it.

"You think he'll stop by?" Hayley asked.

I shook my head. "Why would he?" I snapped. "He

made it clear he wants nothing to do with me."

"Well, I invited Deacon for supper tonight," Lilian said. "I suggested he might bring Grady with."

"Why would you do that?" I propped my hands on my hips as I moved closer to my interfering sister.

"Because he looked like a lovesick man on Thursday."

"Deacon?"

"No, silly. Grady. He loves you, Justine."

I shook my head and picked up the next soaked dress from the basin. Once I fed the bodice through the wringer first, I cranked the handle quickly, catching Hayley unaware.

"A little warning next time," she said as she lunged for the dress before it touched the ground.

I sighed and wiped the sweat off my forehead with my arm.

"I don't really feel like celebrating tonight. Just go out with Deacon."

Lilian stopped scrubbing some undergarments. She studied me for a minute. "But it's your birthday. Are you certain?"

"Positive. Have a delightful date with your man. I'll have a quiet evening with Hay."

Pink tinged Lilian's cheeks. "My man?" she muttered, and shook her head. I noticed the small smile on her lips as she returned to the laundry.

When Deacon arrived for supper, he seemed pleased with the change of plans. He greeted me and Hay before he ushered Lilian out of the house.

I sat down in front of the bowl of stew and slurped it quietly. Hayley must have sensed my mood, as she did not engage in conversation. As I dried the dishes, a knock sounded on the door.

"Justine Harper?"

I nodded.

The young boy thrust a bouquet at me. Then he handed me a small box and a note. As soon as I took the items, he darted off.

"Wait!" I called after him, but he ignored me.

I looked down the street to see if I could spot anyone. Since it was already dark, I couldn't make out anyone in the shadows.

After I closed the door, I set the items on the table.

"What's that?" Hayley asked.

"I don't know."

Then I opened the note and read it. *To my sweet Justine. You are never far from my thoughts. GT.*

A tear slid from the corner of my eye. I pulled the string on the small box. Then I opened it. A gold bracelet glittered in the lamplight. I picked it up and studied the engravings. Swirls danced around daisies. On the inside, letters read: *My love never ends.*

When I set it back in the box, I let tears run down my face. Hayley picked it up and read it.

"From Grady?"

I nodded.

"I told you he still cares for you."

She grabbed my hand and slid the bracelet on it.

"That's where it belongs."

I dried my tears with my handkerchief. When I stood, I stared out the window. I wanted to see him. I wanted him to hold me again. At that moment, the risk didn't matter. Nothing was worse than being separated from him.

On Sunday morning, I donned my bright yellow dress, the same one I wore on my picnic with Grady. It might be a favorite of his. I could not wait for breakfast to finish so we could go to church so I could see Grady. I was positive he would be there.

When we arrived, Deacon slid into the pew next to Lilian. His brother Sam and his children sat behind us with his sister, Vi.

"Where's Grady?" I asked Deacon as the music started playing.

"He's not coming. He and his sister, Ellie Mae, left for Chino Valley yesterday afternoon."

My eyes burned as I spun the bracelet around on my wrist. *Please keep him safe.*

———

LILIAN

When Justine first suggested I go out with Deacon, I refused. It was her birthday. But, as the day wore on and my sister became sullener, I took her suggestion. Weeks passed since Deacon and I had a conversation about something other than the outbreak and subsequent investigation.

"Evening, Lil," he greeted me when I opened the door. After he kissed my cheek, his eyes darted around the table and he frowned.

I quickly explained. "Justine thought we should go out."

Slowly, a smile stretched across his handsome lips. Then it diminished. "But it's her birthday."

"I know. She is not up to company."

His smile returned. "Where would you like to go?"

"Anywhere is fine with me."

I placed my hand in the crook of his arm as we walked toward the main part of town. My heart sped up as I was glad for the time alone with Deacon.

The last time we were alone together was when he obsessively rearranged the furniture in the office. We never spoke about that day. I didn't want to remember the things I wrote in the sheriff's report. I thought Deacon didn't want to remember his odd behavior, either.

When he led me to the same restaurant where we celebrated my birthday, I reached up and touched the earrings he gave me and smiled.

"Will this be alright?"

"Perfect."

The server seated us near the back of the restaurant. He held my chair for me. Then he sat to my right. He sighed as he sat down.

I laid down the menu. "Is something wrong?"

He shook his head. "It seems like a year since we were last here."

I laughed. "I know. It was just two months ago."

He picked up his menu and perused it. "A lot has happen-ed in two months. My mama gave up seeing me at family meals."

I smiled as I imagined the look on his mother's face. "You told her you were busy saving the town, right?"

As he laughed deeply from the belly, my smile widened.

"I told her I was trying to save our beef supply."

After we ordered, Deacon took my hand in his. He rubbed his thumb over my knuckles. "Thanks for inviting me to take you to dinner."

He winked at me.

"Any time."

"I miss this." His voice was a whisper. "Just sitting next to you. No livestock crises. No outlaws threatening us. Just me and you."

When I turned my gaze toward him, his hand released mine. Then it lightly trailed up my arm until it settled at the base of my neck. The air sparked as he leaned closer. He stopped just an inch from my lips.

"Can I kiss you, Lil?"

Heat warmed my face. I nodded my consent.

Then his lips softly brushed against mine. Once. Then twice. Then a third time before he released his hold on me and sat straighter.

A smile stretched across his face. "I could get used to doing that."

When I reached for my iced tea, I let out a shaky breath and I took a sip. My heart echoed his sentiment.

We talked about things unrelated to work. He told me stories about his family. His brother, Boone, sounded like a hoot.

"Then there's my niece, Ashley. She's the cutest little baby I've ever seen." His eyes lit up when he spoke about her.

"Are you around a lot of babies?"

"Most of my brothers have boys. Ashley is the only girl so far. She steals more of my heart every time I hold her."

He sipped his tea and looked away, but not before I caught the longing in his eyes.

"Do you enjoy living on the ranch?"

His gaze refocused on me. "I wouldn't want to live anywhere else. It's home. I know it's far from town, but I don't mind. There is nowhere else that feels so peaceful to me."

"So you never want to live in town?"

"No. It's too noisy and crowded. I..." His words crashed to a halt.

"Deacon, you can tell me anything."

He cleared his throat. Then he studied my face for a good minute before he continued. "It's the only place where

I feel a little normal."

I frowned. "What do you mean?"

He snorted. "Come on, Lil. You've noticed my, um, oddities."

"Like rearranging the furniture at the office?"

Red colored his cheeks, and he looked away. "Yeah, like that."

I reached out and touched his arm. "When life feels out of control, you like to control things. That's not as unusual as you think."

His brown eyes came back to me.

"I am the same way. It's why I was so upset the day we met and you rearranged my brand wall. My life has felt completely out of control for many years. So, I organize things. Things at work. Things at home. My sisters. It makes some part of my heart feel like I have control over something."

"Except we don't really have control over anything, Lil. Only God is in control."

I frowned and looked down at my empty plate before the server removed it. My eyes burned.

"If He's really in control, then why didn't He..."

"Stop Caleb?"

My heart hammered against my chest when he mentioned the man who took far too much from me. More than I had the courage to explain to Deacon. A tear slipped from my eyes.

"I don't know why He didn't stop Caleb. I wish He would have spared you that pain."

I stood.

Deacon quickly tossed some money on the table and followed close behind me as I ran from the building.

"Lil, please, wait."

His hand slid down my arm and clasped mine. Then he drew me close and protected my broken heart with his powerful arms.

The tears flowed and soaked his shirt as I wrapped my arms around his waist.

"Why?" I croaked.

"Shhhh." He stroked a hand over my hair.

"You don't know... The worst of it."

"Lil, just let it out."

My heart shredded as that horrible day tried to fight its way forward from the corner of my memory, where I banished it. The blood. The pain.

Wails escaped from my mouth. I couldn't help it. Deacon guided me to a bench in the town square. He continued to hold me close as the pain from that dark night washed over me like violent torrents of a monsoon rain.

After some time, my sobs slowed. He handed me his handkerchief, and I wiped my face with it.

Then he lifted my chin so he could see my face. He gently ran his fingers along my cheek as he gave me a sympathetic smile. Then he brushed his lips on my forehead before he slid his arm around my shoulders.

He said nothing. He didn't need to. I felt his love. I felt his comfort. I felt his strength.

And I felt his pain. Perhaps he knew about heartbreak. Not the same as mine, but heartbreak nonetheless.

As he escorted me home, I resolved to tell him about that night. I could not do it then. When he learned my darkest secret and greatest failure, I hoped he would still love me.

CHAPTER 19

GRADY

I could have waited until Monday to leave for Chino Valley. Instead, I left on Saturday afternoon, Justine's birthday, because I did not trust myself to stay away from her. Not with that gift. It wasn't the gift I really wanted to give her. That would have to wait until later, when it was safe.

"You're sulking," Ellie Mae said as she rode next to me on her white mare, Moonlight.

"No, I'm not."

She laughed. "You are. And it has nothing to do with this trip, does it?"

I closed my eyes for a second. "It's Justine's birthday."

"Grady!" she squealed. "Why on earth are you taking me to Chino Valley, then?"

I wasn't about to tell my sister Justine's life was in danger because of me. The guilt weighed heavier on my heart. I was putting Ellie Mae in danger, too.

"We need to do this. Let's get it over with and move on."

She angled toward me in her saddle. I kept my gaze fixed firmly on Sunbeam's ears.

"I don't think I believe you, but I'll leave you alone. Me, on the other hand." She laughed. "I needed a break from my little ones."

I snorted. "You love being a mother."

"Sure, I do. But sometimes the constant noise is a bit much. Makes me wonder how Hannah stayed sane with five boys."

She shook her head. "Five, Grady."

I chuckled. "Seems to me like you and Sam are catching up."

We bantered back and forth as we rode. I hadn't realized how long it had been since she and I had just talked without the kids demanding her attention. I enjoyed it.

When we arrived in Chino Valley, we met with the attorney first. He told us that the current tenants were eager to buy the property from us. He promised to draw up the paperwork on Monday.

I led our horses to the hotel and booked rooms for us. Deacon would share my room when he arrived on Sunday evening. He and I planned to investigate the Mason Gang while we were there. Then I took our horses over to the livery.

Ellie Mae wanted to take a nap, so I went to the sheriff's office alone.

"Afternoon," the young man greeted me. If he was older than me, it wasn't by much. "Name's Sheriff Dickerson."

"Grady Thatcher," I introduced myself. "I work with the county livestock inspection office outta Prescott. Do you have a file on the rustlers that came through around six years ago? Murdered a farmer and his wife."

"Well, that'd be before my time. Do you know the farmer's name?"

"Lee and Amy Thatcher."

He narrowed his eyes for a moment. Then he stood and opened a drawer in a file cabinet. He flipped through several files. "Thatcher. Here it is."

When he handed it to me, he said, "It must stay here, but you can read it at that table over there."

After I took the file, I sat at the table, then I opened it and found six pages. That was it. Six pages to document the end of my parents' lives.

I coughed. Then I took a deep breath.

My eyes scanned the sheriff's report. He included my statements about what I witnessed. Another person described the four men who fled the area on horseback. A beefy man dressed all in black. That would be Victor Mason. A younger man in a tan duster with lighter hair. Possibly Caleb Mason. The third man sounded like Amos Thompson. They described the fourth as an older man with a white cowboy hat and two pistols with ivory handles. I did not know his identity.

As I opened my notebook, I wondered who the man was. I copied down the important details despite my shaky hand. The sheriff's report showed that one witness thought the man with the ivory-handled pistols was the leader.

I frowned. I did not know who he was. Clearly, he was not Victor Mason, who, from everything we unearthed, appeared to be the current leader.

Then a thought entered my mind. I wanted to ignore it, for Justine's sake. Could the man be Galen Harper? Victor and Caleb were known associates of his. We knew they frequented Harper's ranch. I wasn't sure I could bring myself to ask Justine if it was her father. Maybe Deacon would talk to Lilian about it.

I pushed the thought away and continued to read the reports. I flipped the page and saw a crude sketch of my family farm. It showed the location where my papa's body was found and where he had been shot. The horses ran some distance, dragging his dead body behind them.

I remembered finding him. His lifeless eyes. His bruised and bloodied body. I bit the inside of my cheek to stem the sorrow.

Shaking my head, I studied the sketch. A mark showed where Mama had been shot. They described the details as I remembered them.

I pinched the bridge of my nose, hoping to keep the tears from coming to the surface. My poor parents' lives had been cut so short. They never got to see Ellie Mae marry Sam. Or hold any of their grandchildren. They would not be there when I married Justine. Oh, how I wished they could be.

It would surprise Papa I became a vet. I was certain he wanted me to farm like he had. If he had not been killed, I would have farmed with him and took over when he grew too old or frail to manage on his own.

Instead, the entire course of my life had been altered by the Mason Gang. So much heartache.

I sighed and flipped through the next few pages. Two were the autopsies of my parents. Go figure, they died of gunshot wounds.

That was it. No other information. No notes on an investigation or suspects. Just myself and two other witnesses.

After I handed the file back to Sheriff Dickerson, I thanked him for his time. Then I mentioned my associate and I might come back on Monday. Of course, I did not know what more we would glean then. Maybe Deacon would have some ideas.

On Sunday morning, Ellie Mae wanted to attend our childhood church. I would have preferred to avoid it, but I went despite my misgivings.

Mrs. Hallstead greeted us and invited us to have supper with her and her husband. We rode out to their place after the service. She and her husband took care of me for a few weeks following my parents' death until Ellie Mae could fetch me. I had been a horrible guest to the kind couple.

"My, you've turned into such a handsome young man," Mrs. Hallstead said as she set out the meal.

"I wanted to thank you for all you did for me. For us. After…" I said.

She placed a hand on my shoulder. "I was glad to help."

I cleared my throat. "Sorry, I was angry and difficult."

Mr. Hallstead waved his hand dismissively. "You were grieving. We understood that."

Mr. Hallstead bowed his head and prayed over the meal. When he finished, I said little. Ellie Mae told them about her marriage and children. Mrs. Hallstead beamed like I imagined Mama would have.

"Your parents would be so proud of you both," she said.

"Thank you, ma'am."

Ellie Mae hugged her and thanked her again for all she had done to help us. Then we left.

Deacon waited for us at the hotel when we returned. He made good time. I escorted Ellie Mae to her room and then Deacon and I headed over to the more popular saloon in town.

I shared what I found with him.

"You think the man with the ivory-handled pistols is Galen Harper?" he asked.

I nodded.

"When we get back, I'll ask Lilian about it. Let's ask around tonight about the four rustlers, and then we'll talk to the sheriff again tomorrow."

"I don't think he knows anything. He's only been the sheriff for a few months."

Deacon rubbed a hand over his chin. "Maybe he knows where we can find the previous sheriff."

The next morning, we headed over to the sheriff's office. Dickerson gave us directions out to Mr. Sloane's property. He was the former sheriff.

We arrived mid-afternoon. I hid a smile as I shook Mr. Sloane's hand. His appearance was like what I remembered. His leathered skin and graying beard fit with his old occupation. Though his waistline had expanded some from when I last saw him.

"Howdy," Sloane greeted us as he invited us in for coffee. "Thatcher, you sure have grown up since I saw you last. How ya been?"

I gave him a few highlights before we got down to business.

"What do you remember about my parents' murder?"

He sighed as he set a mug of thick, black coffee in front of me. Looked more like tar than coffee. He ran a hand over his beard.

"Our only suspects were the rustling gang. After that, no one saw them around. My hands were full with several other cases in town, and I could never do more digging on the case."

I stiffened.

He sighed. "I know that ain't what ya wanted to hear, but it's the truth. Being a sheriff in a growing town ain't easy. They stretched me thin most of the time. I was glad when that kid Dickerson ran against me in the last election. He's got far more stamina than me these days."

"Did you identify any of the gang?" Deacon asked.

"Pretty sure the youngest was Amos Thompson. Folks in

the area knew the Thompson family well. Then there were two brothers. Mason was the last name. Don't recall if I ever got first names for them."

I shook my head. "No names were in the report."

He nodded. "The last one, he owned the unique pistols. Well, a couple of folks thought he had a ranch down near Congress. Never got a name, though. They only remembered him talking about his ranch at a card game. Seemed he had a passel of kids, too."

Deacon's eyes darted to mine. I gave a curt nod. Sure sounded more and more like Galen Harper.

We thanked Sloane for his time and rode back to town. Then we took Ellie Mae to supper at the hotel.

"You're awfully quiet, Grady," she said once our meals arrived.

"Just found out more about the case."

She frowned. "I would love to hear about it."

Deacon cleared his throat. "We think Lilian and Justine's father might have been involved."

My heart pierced to hear the words out loud, even though I already knew they were true.

Ellie Mae sucked in a sharp breath. "Oh, no!"

"We…" I started. "We don't know for sure yet. Let's just keep this between us."

She nodded.

The rest of the supper was somber. After I escorted Ellie Mae to her room, Deacon and I went to the saloon to investigate more. Unfortunately, we came up empty.

I took the couch that night and gave Deacon the bed. I tossed and turned the entire night. When I finally fell asleep, strange dreams haunted me. I dreamed Justine held a gun to my mama's head and laughed mirthlessly as she pulled the trigger.

CHAPTER 20

DEACON

By Tuesday, our business in Chino Valley concluded, and we headed back toward Colter Ranch. Grady and Ellie Mae signed all the paperwork to sell their farm. Both seemed sad and relieved to leave that part of their lives behind.

As we rode, my mind turned over the details of all we had learned. Sounded like Galen Harper was the leader of the Mason Gang. I doubted Lilian would be surprised, though I thought she might feel guilty that her family played a part in destroying Grady's. I prayed she would not take that on herself.

"Deacon." Grady got my attention. He nodded toward a plume of dust in the distance.

I reached into my saddlebags and found my field glasses. I stopped Sergeant as Grady and Ellie Mae continued on. As I looked through the glass, I confirmed there were rustlers in the distance. Four men. One in all black. They were too far away to see other details clearly.

I clicked my tongue to nudge Sergeant to catch up to Grady.

"Think it's the Mason Gang."

Grady frowned.

"Get your sister out of here. Ride hard until you don't see them anymore."

"No. I want to follow them."

"Grady, your first responsibility is your family."

I watched as the conflict warred on his face. At length, he nodded.

"I'll hide in that wash over there." I pointed to it. "Follow it closer to them. Then I'll figure out if it's safe for me to follow them further."

"We need to find their hiding place."

"I'll do my best. You just get Ellie Mae home safely."

"I'll come back for you."

I shook my head. "No, don't do that. I'll contact you when I know more. They'll be gone from here before you could make it back."

I turned Sergeant toward the dry wash bed as Grady's voice stopped me.

"You're like a brother to me, Deacon. Don't go and get yourself killed."

My fingers touched the brim of my hat in acknowledgment. I heard the fear in his voice. I'd feel the same if our roles were reversed.

Grady urged Ellie Mae to press her horse for speed. I watched the Mason Gang from a safe distance until Grady and Ellie Mae's horses' hoofbeats faded.

Then I followed the wash, periodically stopping to make sure I'd be able to catch up to the Mason Gang. As dusk fell over the desert, they stopped and made camp. Fortunately for me, the wash still provided suitable cover, so I camped there and gave Sergeant a break from wearing the saddle.

Before night fell, I peered through the field glasses again.

I studied the brands. Franks. Gardner. Colter. They stole from my family.

I stowed my gear and settled in for the night as I thought through my next move. If I continued to follow them under the cover of the wash, I might find their hiding place. Or I could return to Prescott and gather others. If I did that, though, we probably wouldn't find them again.

As I laid down to sleep, I decided I best continue to follow them as long as I could.

Just before dawn, a noise woke me. The low moan of cattle sounded closer than the night before. I crawled quietly on my belly toward the top of the wash. I set my hat aside and carefully peered over the edge. The herd came closer to my position than the night before.

I quickly ducked down once I assessed the situation. They drove the cattle my way, assuming there was water in the wash. There wasn't, but they didn't know that.

After I grabbed my gear, I slung the saddle onto Sergeant's back without securing it. Then I led him back the way we came until a bend hid me. I cinched the saddle in place and double checked everything in case I needed to get out of there quickly.

Then I waited. And waited some more. The noise of the herd faded. I peered around the bend. They were gone.

Suddenly, a noise came from above me.

"Well, if it ain't Lilian Harper's new beau."

I spun to face Caleb Mason and drew my pistol at the same time. Something hit my head hard from my blind spot and I went to the ground before darkness swallowed me.

———

DEACON

I sat up in the wash and took stock of my situation. The sun hung low in the sky. I was miles from anywhere. My canteen lay next to my legs. I still had my gun belt and both guns. A hat. A pounding headache. Not much else. I stood up and steadied myself by leaning against the wall of the wash as dizziness threatened to steal my balance.

When I felt sure on my feet again, I slowly looked around. Sergeant was nowhere. My blood boiled.

There were three things if you stole or harmed that guaranteed a stockman would hunt you down: his woman, his horse, or his cattle. They hurt my woman. They took my horse. And they stole my brother's cattle. They better believe I was coming after them.

I took a sip from my canteen and walked through the wash back toward civilization. It would take a long time on foot, so I tried to figure out where the closest road was. The new Santa Fe, Prescott, & Phoenix Railway line was probably the closest way to get anywhere, but I didn't think they would stop and let me on it.

My shoulders sagged. Best bet was to walk back toward Chino Valley. I sent a prayer heavenward for the strength to make it, or for God to intervene and send someone to help.

I followed the wash into the night. The moon provided enough light for me to press on despite my aching feet. I walked until I was too exhausted to go any further.

Then I laid down and slept in the dust of the dry wash.

The next morning, I woke to the sound of a squeaky wagon. I jumped to my feet and climbed up the side of the wash. An old miner with a wagon full of gear drove at a slow pace. I waved my arms and shouted. He stopped and turned around in his seat. Then he waved back and waited for me to catch up.

"Where you headed?" I asked.

"Prescott. Mister, you alright?"

"They robbed me on the way home and stole my horse."

The miner smiled sympathetically. "Climb on up. We ain't fast, but we're a mite better'n walking."

I thanked him for his kindness.

"What's your name?" he asked.

"Deacon Colter."

He raised an eyebrow. "Any relation to Boone?"

"He's my older brother."

"Well, if that don't beat all. I worked a job with him a few years ago on Mike Fremont's crew. Name's Clancey Smith."

I smiled. "Pleasure to meet you."

The rest of the ride into town, Clancey regaled me with tales of Boone's risky adventures when they surveyed a route for the mines in the Bradshaw Mountains. It was fun learning a few stories about my wild big brother.

When the town came into view, I had him drop me at the livestock inspection office. Then I thanked him for his help.

As I turned the knob to open the door, I heard Grady's harsh words to Lilian. It was the only time I thought I might fight my best friend if I had the energy.

CHAPTER 21

LILIAN

"He should have contacted us by now," Grady said, while he paced back and forth across the length of the lobby.

My heart squeezed tight. I was as worried as he was about the lack of contact from Deacon. It had been two days since Grady left him alone in the desert to follow the Masons.

"Calm down. He can take care of himself," Perry reminded us.

"We should go after him. Something is wrong."

"You're making me nervous," I said as I wrung my hands.

Grady stopped. His scowl was inconsistent with the man that loved my sister.

"We should ride to Harper Ranch to see if your father has him."

I leaned back in my chair. "My father? What does he have to do with anything?"

"It's his gang. Victor, Caleb, and Amos work for him."

"Hold up," Perry said, as he gently nudged Grady away

from my desk. "You said nothing about Harper."

Grady kicked at the leg of a chair. "The fourth man in the gang is the leader. An older man who bragged about having a passel of children. He lives on a ranch down near Congress."

Could be my papa. Could be two other ranchers in the area. I waited silently for Grady to continue.

"Wears a pair of ivory-handled six shooters."

My throat tightened. I closed my eyes. I could see them. One on each of Papa's hips. No one else in a hundred miles had guns like those. I slowly opened my eyes to Grady's frown.

"See?" Grady said as he pointed at me. "Just look at her reaction. She knows it's Galen Harper."

I nodded as I tried to calm my racing heart. "It sounds like him."

Perry frowned. Then he told Grady to sit down. "Don't need you flying off the handle and getting yourself in over your hot head."

I flattened my hands on the top of my desk. Then I rubbed them in lines, almost as if I was smoothing out fabric.

When I looked up, both Perry and Grady stared at me. I took a deep breath and shared the contents of the letter I received from Shane a few days ago.

"My brother, Shane, said Papa left a few weeks ago. He's not expected back for a while. Something about needing to unload some diseased cattle."

Grady growled. "They were the ones that brought the foot and mouth cattle to town, weren't they?"

"I don't know!" I hollered as I stood and placed my hands on my hips. "Shane didn't say."

"Go on," Perry encouraged me.

"He said they were planning to replace the forty head they lost. It was all he knew. It sounded like he was getting concerned for my youngest brothers. He kept hinting that it might be nice for them to see their sisters in Prescott soon."

"Maybe we ought to take a trip down to see your brothers," Grady growled.

I frowned. "Leave them out of this!"

"I'm not the one that brought them into this!"

The door flew open.

"Deacon!" His name rushed from my lips as he collapsed into a chair.

He wiped the sweat from his forehead with his sleeve. Dust and dirt clung to every bit of his exposed skin except for where dried blood crusted the side of his face.

My breath caught, and I froze for a few seconds. Water. He needed water. And a doctor.

I rushed to the sink and filled a pitcher with water. Then I filled a glass and handed it to him. He gulped it down. I poured him another.

"Thank you, Lil."

My heart warmed for a second before I hurried away to dampen a cloth. Then I rushed to his side and dabbed at the dried blood.

"We need to get you to a doctor," I said through my tight throat.

"I'm fine. A bump is all."

I snorted. "What happened?"

"They found me and knocked me out. Stole Sergeant."

A shadow fell across his face.

"Who?" I asked.

"Caleb Mason was talking to me when someone else caught me off guard. I'm pretty sure Victor was there, too."

"Anyone else?" Grady asked.

Deacon glanced at me for a second before he responded. "The man with the ivory-handled pistols."

My knees felt weak. I hit the chair with a thud as the wind left me.

"Galen Harper," Grady spat out my father's name.

Deacon nodded.

Tears burned my eyes. My father hurt Deacon. Stole his horse. Left him for dead.

"They had some Colter cattle in the mix. A few other regis-tered brands."

Perry cleared his throat. "Let's clean you up. Go to the doctor. We'll figure out the next course of action."

Grady's anger kept him from being helpful, so I accompanied Deacon to the doctor. I needed to be sure he was alright.

I sat beside Deacon as the doctor examined him.

"You likely had a concussion," the doctor said, "but I don't see any reason to keep you. You're already on the mend."

As the doctor left the exam room, Deacon said, "Lil, I'm sorry."

"What are you sorry for?"

"That your father is involved."

I sighed. "I'm just glad he or his gang didn't kill you or kidnap you."

He placed a hand on the small of my back and ushered me from the room. When we stepped out into the bright sunlight, he squinted.

"You should go home and rest," I said.

He grunted. "Too much to be done."

"Deacon, you won't do anyone any good if you collapse."

"Maybe I could borrow your couch for a bit?"

I sighed. "Fine. It's about suppertime, anyway. I suppose I could feed you. Least I could do since my family is the one that did this to you."

He laced his fingers with mine as we walked to my house.

"This isn't your fault or your responsibility, Lil. Your father has done this all on his own."

"I know that." I answered too quickly. My mind knew it wasn't my fault, but that didn't stop my heart from feeling guilty.

I opened the door to my house. Hayley already had supper going, so I sat in a chair near Deacon while he reclined on the couch. He fell asleep for twenty minutes before supper was ready. When Hayley set out the meal, I woke him.

A knock sounded on the door. I stood and opened it.

"Grady!" Justine ran to him and pulled him into an embrace. At first he looked stiff, then he melted into her hold.

I sat at the table to allow them privacy. They joined us, and Justine's face remained bright throughout the meal.

When supper finished, Deacon pulled me aside. Then he placed his hands on my waist. "Do you want to come with us tomorrow down to Harper Ranch to check on your brothers?"

"Is it safe for me?"

"I don't think so, but I'd rather you ride with us than sneak down there on your own."

"I'll stay here, I promise."

He pulled me close, and I rested my head against his chest as my arms tightened around his middle.

"Good." His voice reverberated in his chest.

When I sniffed, he lifted my chin and his deep brown eyes studied my face.

"I'm glad you're alright. I thought the worst, you

know," I whispered as a few tears moistened my cheeks.

"I'm sorry, Lil."

Then he leaned closer and brushed his lips across mine. The kiss was far too brief, but he communicated so much. He missed me. He loved me.

Oh, how I loved him.

"I'll see you in the morning," he promised, before he left with Grady.

———

JUSTINE

The last person I expected to see at supper was Grady. When he showed up on our doorstep, all rational thought left my brain. I ran to him and wrapped him in my arms.

At first, he seemed uncomfortable. Then he relaxed and pulled me closer. He kissed me in a way that chased away all my doubts about him. When he finally pulled away and my breath slowed, I asked him, "Did you mean what you had engraved on the bracelet?"

His eyes revealed his heart to me. He meant it. He loved me.

"Very much."

It was hard not to smile throughout the entire meal. He was there, by my side. In the flesh. The man I loved.

My joy faded as he and Deacon shared their plans.

"We're gonna head down toward Congress tomorrow," Grady said. "See if we can find the men Deacon was following."

I frowned. "Are you going to Harper Ranch?"

Grady's jaw tightened. "Can't say."

"Or won't?" I asked. I glanced at Lilian, and she looked away.

"Lilian," I said, "Tell me the truth. Are they going to our ranch?"

She gave a slight nod.

"You better not hurt Shane or Flynn or Ike." My eyes locked with Grady's. "Promise me."

"We have no issue with your brothers. As long as they stay out of the way, they will have nothing to worry about."

"That's not the answer I'm looking for. Promise me they will be alright."

Grady shook his head. "I can't promise that. For all I know, they are in on this, too."

I frowned as Deacon stood and led Lilian away from the table. When Hayley rose and began clearing the dishes, I turned my ire on Grady.

"You can't be serious. You can't believe that my younger brothers are involved. Flynn is sixteen and Ike is only four-teen."

Grady looked away. "It would surprise you what a four-teen-year-old is capable of."

I grabbed his arm. "Look at me."

I narrowed my eyes. "I guarantee that Flynn and Ike have nothing to do with this. They are as innocent as me or Hayley or Lilian. Our only crime is that we were born to a horrible man."

Grady stood and walked to the door.

"Grady, please don't leave angry at me," I pleaded.

"I need to go."

He opened the door and walked out. Deacon followed behind him.

As the tears flowed, I ran to my room and flopped down on my bed. His anger destroyed any happiness I had.

"Justine?" Lilian said from the doorway. "What's wrong?"

I shook my head. "He actually believes that Shane, Flynn, and Ike could somehow be part of this."

Lilian sat on the edge of the bed. "He's upset. He just learned our father ordered his parents' murder."

I bolted upright. "What?!"

She nodded solemnly. "Papa had Grady's parents murder-ed."

My heart shredded into tiny pieces at the news. No wonder he was angry.

"Imagine if you were in his boots. The father of the woman he loves took his family from him. He was fifteen when it happened."

My tears flowed again. Lilian hugged me for several minutes until I calmed down.

"I wished we had been born into some other family."

Lilian snorted. "Wishing it doesn't make it so."

I resolved to pray for Deacon, Grady, their mission, and the safety of my brothers. I hoped the next time I saw him, he would be the man I fell in love with and not the bitter, angry man that sat at my supper table.

CHAPTER 22

DEACON

By the time I got home, I was bone weary, but I drew a bath, anyway. So glad we had indoor plumbing put in last year. I eased myself into the warm water, which instantly turned murky from all the dust I'd collected over the past few days.

A part of me longed to be done with the livestock inspection job. I missed my quiet life as the vet at the stockyards. Derek had yet to replace me. Perhaps we could bring in the Mason Gang soon.

Lilian's smile came to mind. I pictured her sitting across from me at the dining room table in my house. I wanted her in my life. If, after courting, she wanted me, then I would ask her to be my wife. It was too soon for such thoughts, but my heart desired it. For the first time, I believed that one woman, Lil, saw past my odd compulsive behavior to the real me.

I sighed and dipped my head in the murky water. Then I scrubbed the filth from my hair before I stood and toweled off as the tub drained.

After I rinsed out the tub, I retired to my room. Only

my mind wouldn't let me sleep. I worked through potential scenarios about what could unfold at Harper Ranch. We could not know what lay ahead. Neither Grady nor I were familiar with the property. We knew only what Lilian and Justine said about their brothers, and their descriptions were rose-colored.

A fitful night's sleep left me in a solemn mood the next day. I missed my horse and did not look forward to picking out one to borrow. Relief washed over me when I ran into my Uncle Adam in the barn before breakfast.

"Deacon, I didn't see Sergeant in his stall. I thought you were still gone."

"They stole him." I fisted a hand at my side as anger simmered. I prayed Sergeant was safe.

"I'm so sorry. Suppose you're looking for a new horse."

"Just to borrow. I'm hoping to get him back soon."

Adam walked along the stalls until he came to one near the end of the stables. "I've got this four-year-old gelding here. Reminds me a lot of Sergeant when he was younger."

I frowned. A brown gelding. Not a blood bay. Not my Sergeant.

"He's a good cattle horse. Sure on his feet on the trail. Excellent endurance. Smart too."

As I faced the stall, I studied him. His brown coat glistened with a hint of gold. The white blaze on his face gave him some character. When he moved closer, he snorted and hung his head over the stall gate. Then he nudged my arm with his nose. I gave him a half-smile as I rubbed his blaze. His ears flicked.

Adam held up a bucket of oats, and I offered the horse some from my hand. He took them and nodded his head. Yup. The horse nodded his head at me.

"What's his name?"

"Your aunt wanted to call him Coffee. But I call him Bear."

I quirked an eyebrow. "Bear?"

Bear nudged my arm again. I supposed he was alright. "Howdy, Bear."

He snorted.

Uncle Adam laughed. "He likes you."

"Guess I'll borrow him. I'll need a saddle and tack too."

"Go on up for breakfast and I'll get him ready for you."

I thanked my uncle.

As soon as breakfast was over, Grady and I headed into town. I returned the horse I had rented yesterday. The one normal part of my day was walking to Lilian's house to escort her to work.

"Morning." She smiled as she stepped onto the porch.

Then she drew closer until she stood in front of me. She took another step, leaving no space between us. My heart thrummed as she placed a hand on my chest. When she played with a button on my shirt, I took a deep breath. She smelled like a cool spring morning.

"I missed you," she whispered. "I'm glad you came back in one piece."

She tilted her head back until her blue eyes searched mine. Then I placed a hand on the small of her back, and she slid her arms around my neck.

"Are you going to stand there all morning, Deacon? Or are you going to kiss me?"

I obliged my woman and lowered my lips to hers. As she returned the kiss, she stirred a feeling deep within me, like I belonged with her forever. At length, I slowed the kiss, then ended it softly.

She looked away. "Please stay safe."

"Lil. Look at me."

She turned her gaze to me.

"I will do my best to stay safe. I want nothing more than to come back to you."

Lilian wrapped her arms around my middle and squeezed. Too soon, she left my arms and let out a slow breath.

"We best be on our way. Let's not be late for work."

I laughed as I laced my fingers with hers. "Yes, ma'am."

As we walked, she spoke softly, "If my brothers aren't safe, would you send them here? I have this feeling, like they need me."

"I promise."

"Thank you."

Grady coughed as we walked past him. "If you're finished saying your goodbyes, we best be on our way."

I waited for Lilian to open the office. Then I touched my fingertips to my hat brim. When she smiled, I let the door close. Then I mounted Bear.

Grady and I wound down the mountain road in silence. Once we rode along the valley floor, he spoke.

"I was thinking maybe Warren Cahill would let us stay at his place."

"Good idea. I suppose he's fairly close to the Harper spread."

It was lunchtime when we arrived. Warren was out with the herd, along with his grown son, Nathan.

"Deacon, Grady!" Aunt Mary greeted us warmly. "What brings you to the valley?"

Grady explained as she offered us a simple meal. "We were hoping you might let us use your place as our base while we investigate at a nearby ranch."

"Of course. Nathan will be excited to see you. And I'm sure Warren won't mind."

We thanked her for the meal and promised to come back before nightfall, even though it was possible we might not be. We headed west and rode for another hour before we came to Harper's land.

Broken down wagons, a rusted plow, and dilapidated outbuildings lined the roadside. The barn had to be the sturdiest building on the property. One stiff monsoon wind might blow the house to the ground.

"Did the girls really live here?" I muttered. I hoped it had been in better shape then.

Bear's ears perked up. I scanned the area. A man stood in the barn's shadow. I nodded to Grady. He saw him, too.

We rode in that direction. I kept one hand near my pistol as we reined in.

"Good afternoon!" Grady called out.

A thin young man stepped from the shadows, holding a shotgun. He pointed it at Grady's chest.

"What you want?" A scowl etched his face.

"Flynn?" I guessed his name. Lilian said he was sixteen. I couldn't tell if the bag of bones was sixteen or not.

"How do you know my name?"

He pointed the gun at me.

"I'm a friend of your sisters. Lilian, Justine, and Hayley."

He frowned as he stepped fully into the sunlight. "You saw Lilian?"

"Just this morning."

"Is Shane around or your papa?" Grady asked.

"Shane will be back soon. Just me and Ike." He jerked his head toward the house.

"Mind pointing that shotgun somewhere else?" I asked.

He lowered it to the ground, and I breathed easier. I slowly dismounted. As soon as my feet hit the dirt, he hurried over to me.

"How is Lilian? Did she say anything about us? Can we go live with her?"

My heart broke at the desperation in the kid's voice.

"She's doing good. She's a secretary at an office."

"Justine is working at the dry goods store," Grady added. "And Hayley works at a law office."

Flynn straightened his back and sniffed. "They're safe?"

"Yeah. Safe and happy."

His shoulders slumped.

"Hey!" a man on horseback shouted.

"It's okay, Shane. They know Lilian," Flynn said as Shane pulled his horse up next to us.

"What's your business here?" Shane stayed on his horse and fingered his pistol handle.

"My name is Grady. This is Deacon. We don't mean any trouble. We work for the county and we're here to inspect the cattle. Hopefully, it wouldn't be too much trouble if we looked around."

Shane stiffened. "I don't think that's a good idea."

"We recently had an outbreak of foot and mouth disease. Me and Deacon are veterinarians. Our boss sent us here, so you'd be doing us a favor if we could inspect the health of your herd."

Grady never ceased to amaze me. Trying to convince the young man he'd be helping us.

"Our boss will be pretty upset with us if we come back without doing our job."

Shane frowned. Then he dismounted.

"Only got about twenty head. They're corralled out back."

"Oh?" I asked. "I thought Lilian said you typically ran around fifty to a hundred."

"Yeah, well, our father," his tone turned acidic, "took

most of what we had and left us a handful of underweight, weak animals."

Grady chatted up Shane while we headed to the corral, continuing to build trust with him. When we rounded the corner and saw the cattle, I understood Shane's frustration. He'd not be able to sell what he had. Weren't worth the cost of feeding.

Ike joined his brothers and watched as I inspected the malnourished animals. No signs of disease. They were severely underweight and in danger of dying from starvation within the month.

"Run out of feed?" I asked.

"Months ago," Shane said.

"Papa hasn't brought anymore," Flynn said. "Nothing for us either."

"You think about letting them loose to find grass?" Grady asked.

"Papa doesn't like them to run free. Even if I did, there ain't much grass this season. Been too dry."

"Can we go see Lilian in Prescott?" Ike said. "I miss her. She always made sure we had food."

Shane placed a hand on his shoulder. "I don't have no money to send you anywhere."

Grady cleared his throat. "You're in luck, kiddo. Lilian sent some money with us for stage fare."

It was a lie. I'd pay for the fare, but it didn't matter where the money came from. These boys needed a hearty meal and a reliable roof over their head. With their sunken eyes and bony limbs, they looked about as good as the dying cattle.

"We need to head back to a friend's ranch," I said. "But if you'd like to come with us, we can send you on the stage in the morning."

"Can we Shane?" Ike pleaded.

"You two go on. Papa won't like it if I'm not here when he gets back."

Grady pulled Shane aside as I suggested the boys gather anything they wanted to take with them. They both said everything that they owned was already on them. My stomach churned over their poverty. Galen Harper was a terrible man.

"Alright, boys, let's go," Grady said.

Ike rode with me and Flynn with Grady.

When we arrived at Aunt Mary's place, both Nathan and Warren headed in for the night. They greeted us and asked about the boys. Grady explained while I took care of our horses.

By the time I entered the house, the boys already looked cleaner. I smiled. Aunt Mary preferred a tidy face at her supper table.

We filled the meal with conversation about our family. Aunt Mary asked dozens of questions about Mama, Papa, Vi, and my brothers and their families.

I watched as Aunt Mary piled huge amounts of food on the boys' plates for a second helping. They ate as if they hadn't eaten in days. I was glad we came if for no other reason than to send those boys to someone who would love them and care for their wellbeing.

"Thank you, Mrs. Cahill," Ike said. "I ain't had so much food since Lilian left."

I'd omit that tidbit the next time I spoke to Lilian. She didn't need to feel guilty for leaving her brothers behind, though I knew she would.

After supper, Nathan occupied the boys while Grady and I spoke with Warren in his den.

"I have some money," I said, "to put them on the stage

tomorrow morning. Send them to their sisters' place in Prescott. Would you mind taking them into town?"

"Sure," Warren said. "Nathan or I will be happy to."

"Shane gave his permission for us to come back tomorrow," Grady said. "He expects Galen to be gone for a few more days. That gives us time to look around the property."

"And to convince him to leave, too," I said. "He looks as bad off as the younger boys."

"Lilian said he's older than you, Deacon."

"Doesn't look it. He looks sickly."

"Mary will pack food for tomorrow. Be sure to give the young man plenty," Warren said.

We thanked Warren for his help. Then we headed out to the barn to sleep in the loft. Flynn and Ike took the spare bed in the house.

As I laid staring up at the barn ceiling, I prayed for the Harper boys. They lived a hard life and they need their sisters. I prayed they would never have to go back to that place.

CHAPTER 23

GRADY

The next morning, when we arrived at Harper Ranch, Shane greeted us.

"You had breakfast yet?" I asked.

When he shook his head, I dug in the saddlebags, and I handed him two biscuits overstuffed with eggs and bacon. He slowly nibbled on one while we entered the barn.

The stalls were properly cleaned. Everything looked well cared for, including the two horses. Guess Galen took better care of his horses than his sons.

"What's behind that door?" Deacon asked. He pointed toward a room with a padlock on it.

"Um… That's Papa's place. I ain't allowed to go in there."

"Do you have a key?" I asked.

He shook his head.

I stepped closer to Deacon and kept my voice low. "We need to get in there."

Deacon studied the lock. "I think I can pry the latch from the wood. You distract him."

"Shane," I said as I placed my hand on his shoulder. "I

hate to ask, but could I trouble you for some coffee?"

I directed him out of the barn. "I brought some grounds, so I just need to borrow your stove and coffeepot."

"Alright."

I retrieved the grounds from my saddlebags. Then he led me up to the house. As we waited for the coffee to boil, I glanced around the house.

Dust coated every surface. Several broken chairs lined the table. The ladder to the loft had split rungs. Three mats rested on the dirty floor in the next room. My heart broke. No wonder Justine was positive her brothers had nothing to do with her father's work. They lived in squalor.

I bit the inside of my cheek as I pictured Lilian, Justine, and Hayley living in such destitute circumstances.

"The place always look like this?"

"No. Lilian and Justine made it home. As much as they could. I don't have enough energy to tend to everything."

His voice caught.

"Spend most days trying to find food. Desert quail. Heck, I've trapped a few desert hares. Anything to put food in their bellies."

He slouched in a chair as I poured us both some coffee. He savored the liquid. "Been a long time since I've had coffee."

"Why'd you stay?"

Shane looked out the dirty window. "My papa threatened more'n once to hunt me down and kill me if I left. If I was dead, what would happen to Flynn and Ike?"

"They made it on the morning stage. They'll reunite with your sisters in a few hours."

I sipped my coffee.

"You know," I said, "with them gone, there's no reason for you to stay. Ride back with us."

"But what if Papa hunts me down?"

"He can't do anything to you in town. Too many people. I imagine your papa does his best to avoid attention in a situation like that."

We both sipped our coffee. Then I stood and poured a cup for Deacon.

"Let's take this out to Deacon."

Shane led the way back to the barn.

When we arrived, Deacon sat at a desk in the secret room. Papers covered the entire surface of the desk.

Shane frowned, but he didn't confront us. He sat on a nice cushioned chair and watched as we read through the papers.

"Grady, look at this."

Deacon handed me a piece of paper. B. Irving. My heart pounded as I scanned the paper, then flipped through the next several. A deed for a property some twenty miles from Harper Ranch.

"Hey, Shane, are you familiar with this place?" I asked as I handed him the deed.

He cleared his throat. "Papa had me ride out there once to pick up some cattle."

He looked away. "It wasn't ours. I refused to go the next time."

"You think you could draw us a map?"

He nodded. I scrounged around until I found some paper and a pencil. Shane pulled a side table close to his chair and worked on the map while Deacon and I sorted through the other papers.

"Look." I handed Deacon a page with sketches of a dozen brands. Colter. Larson. Thompson. Gardner. Franks. Several others.

Deacon placed it in a pile, where he collected evidence

against Galen Harper and the Mason Gang.

Several branding irons stood in a corner. Brands altered from the ones we found on the papers. Slight variations that'd fool anyone not looking closely.

We found even more evidence. Falsified paperwork. Bills of sale. Chain of custody. All signed by B. Irving.

"Shane? You know who B. Irving is?"

"That's Papa's alias."

I sucked in a sharp breath at the matter-of-fact way he said it. We had to convince Shane to leave for Prescott, where he'd be protected. He was a better witness than we first realized.

After a few more hours, we gathered the branding irons and paperwork. We packed them on our horses.

Then I finally convinced Shane to come with us. He mounted his horse and rode with us back to the Cahills.

Aunt Mary treated him as well as she had his brothers.

"I was wondering," Nathan said at supper. "I'm heading to Prescott for some supplies. Shane, would you like to ride up with me? Make sure your brothers made it alright."

"Tomorrow? On a Sunday?"

"We'll have to wait until Monday, but you can stay with us if you like."

"I... I suppose I could."

I breathed a sigh of relief.

The next morning, despite it being the Lord's Day, Deacon and I headed out to B. Irving's property using the map Shane made. As we neared the place, plumes of dust floated in the air.

We stopped in a wash which we used as cover. Deacon looked through his field glasses before handing it to me.

Hundreds of cattle dotted the land. The brands matched the sketches we discovered. Horses too. I scanned the horses and found Sergeant.

"Deacon, your horse."

I handed him the field glasses, and he spotted him.

"Thank God. He's still alive."

We watched the property for an hour from the cover of our hiding spot.

"There are too many men. We can't go in there alone," I said.

"Yeah. We need to wire Perry to bring the sheriff and a posse."

I agreed. We backtracked on foot until we were out of sight of the ranch. Then we rode back to Cahills. I continued into Congress and the telegraph station and waited for the reply.

"Be there tomorrow."

I took the message back to Deacon.

As we retired for the night, my mind raced. After six long years, I had my parents' murderers in sight. I would bring them in and get justice for my family.

CHAPTER 24

LILIAN

On Saturday morning, Justine started our laundry. I headed to the mercantile to purchase food and supplies for the week. I smiled as I thought about how far we'd come in the six months since we left Harper Ranch behind.

All three of us were healthy. We had a safe home. Our jobs put a roof over our heads, food in our bellies, and left some funds for new purchases, like clothing.

When we first moved to Prescott, as soon as I was able, I bought a new dress and tossed the old one in the rag bin. I did the same for my sisters.

A stab of guilt pierced my heart. The conditions at the ranch were appalling. I hoped Deacon and Grady would not judge me too harshly for leaving my brothers behind. They didn't want to leave with Justine and Hayley. Still, I should have written to Shane to pester him about sending them. I was certain things got worse after I left. Justine told me countless times that I was the rock that held the family together.

I stopped as the stagecoach drove past me. Then I crossed the street to the mercantile.

"Lilian!"

A bony boy ran toward me. I blinked as recognition dawn-ed.

"Ike!"

He launched himself into my arms. Within seconds, Flynn did the same thing.

"We missed you," Flynn said as he straightened. His eyes misted, then he lifted his chin and frowned.

"We met Deacon and Grady," Ike said. "They said you sent money to bring us here."

I smiled. I would pay Deacon back as soon as I could. Right then, I needed to purchase clothes and shoes for my brothers. And food.

"I'm going to the store. Would you like to join me?"

They both nodded.

When we entered the store, I dragged them to the clothing section. I held a shirt in front of Flynn. He scowled but humored me. I picked something oversized, as I hoped he would bulk up after a few months of solid food. Then I did the same for Ike.

Once we figured out their sizes, I asked them to pick two shirts and pants each. Then I asked the clerk to size them for shoes while I shopped for food. I tripled the amount of food I planned to buy.

The final tally concerned me. Thankfully, Justine was due her pay at the end of the coming week. I knew I could purchase against our account, but I hated to do so.

The boys carried most of the purchases for me. While I held the door to our small house open, they entered.

"It's so big!" Ike's jaw gaped as he set the purchases on the table.

"I suppose it is," I said as I thought back to the cramped, rundown home on the ranch.

"Hello!" I called out. My sisters came in from the back-yard. "Look who I found."

My brothers and sisters excitedly greeted each other with hugs all around. Justine's face clouded when she looked at me. I knew she thought they were too thin.

"I know it's early but would you boys like some lunch?" she asked.

They both nodded.

Hayley and I put away the groceries while Justine fixed some sandwiches with meat leftover from last night's supper. Then I placed their clothes on Hayley's bed.

Hayley moved her things into Justine's room while our brothers ate.

"Mrs. Cahill made us bacon *and* sausage for breakfast," Ike exclaimed. "She was so nice to us and fed us real good."

I smiled. "We will mail her a thank you note."

When the boys finished eating, Hayley drew a bath.

"Ike, you're up first," she said.

His eyes rounded. "You have indoor plumbing!"

She laughed. "It's nice. I think you'll like it."

He started stripping down, and Hayley quickly stepped out of the bathroom and closed the door behind her.

"Please tell me you bought some clothes for them," Justine said.

"Yes, I laid them out in Hayley's old room."

She grabbed a set of the smaller clothes and placed them outside the bathroom door. "Looks like he was so excited to bathe, he forgot them."

"How is Shane?" Justine asked Flynn.

"Stubborn as ever." Flynn crossed his arms over his chest.

I kept my voice light. "He let you and Ike come here, didn't he?"

"Yeah. Well, I was gonna bring Ike as soon as Deacon

175

and Grady said you sent for us. Don't matter what he thought."

When Ike joined us in the parlor, Hayley started toward the bathroom. Flynn pushed her aside.

"Hey!" she squawked at him. "What was that for?"

"I'm not a boy. I can draw a bath for myself." He ducked into his new room and grabbed a change of clothes. Then he stormed into the bathroom and slammed the door shut.

Hayley frowned. "I was just trying to help."

I sighed and sank onto the couch. I patted the spot next to me, and Ike hurried to it.

"Oh, I forgot." He stood and ran into his bedroom. A minute later, he returned with an envelope, which he handed to me. "Deacon said to give this to you."

As he sat next to me again, I opened the envelope.

> Dearest Lil,
>
> Sorry, I wasn't able to get Shane to leave. Grady and I will search the place tomorrow, so I'm sure Grady will keep working on him. We have a solid lead on the gang's whereabouts.
>
> Looking forward to holding you in my arms again soon.
>
> All my love,
>
> DC

All my love. I prayed he would stay safe and come back to me soon.

———

JUSTINE

When my brothers showed up, relief filled my heart. I was grateful to Deacon and Grady for getting them out of there. Thankfully, my father had not been at the ranch when they arrived.

I would have worried about Grady more, but my brothers' presence upset the peaceful balance of our home. Anger emanated from Flynn. He begrudgingly went to church with us on Sunday. Then he sulked and tried to pick fights with Hayley.

When he shoved Hayley after Sunday supper, I intervened.

"Listen, mister," I said as I grabbed his ear like Mama used to do when we were bad as children. "You're bigger than her. Don't treat a woman like that. If you do, I'll toss you out."

He brushed my hand away and narrowed his eyes. "Who says?"

"I do," Lilian said.

Flynn stepped in front of her. He grew since I last saw him. Now he stood head and shoulders above Lilian. "I don't care what you say. You abandoned us."

"Flynn," Hayley said. "That's not fair. It was more dangerous for us."

Flynn snorted. "Yeah, well, it ain't no fun to starve while you lived it up in this place."

He stormed out of the house. I started after him, but Lilian stopped me.

"Let him go. He'll come back."

"How can you be so sure?"

"Because he knows how good living here is."

I sighed.

Hayley added, "He's not used to having any rules. And Papa was a horrible example. It's gonna take time for him to settle down."

"I suppose so."

"Lilian," Ike said. "I'm glad you sent for us. I like it here."

She smiled and gave him a side hug. "You want to help me with the dishes?"

He nodded.

I held back a sigh as I cleared the table. At least Ike appreciated his new home.

A pang of nostalgia hit me as I watched him. He adored Lilian, who was a solid ten years older than him. Growing up, Lilian acted as our mother long before Mama passed on. He didn't remember Mama. She filled that void for him. Lilian took care of him as long as he could remember.

"Do you need me to do anything else, Lilian? I'll help with whatever I can. Just don't leave me again."

Tears burned my eyes as Ike buried his head in Lilian's shoulder. He stood as tall as her.

"Hush now. You aren't going anywhere. You're here to stay," Lilian comforted him.

Around suppertime, Flynn returned. He said nothing. After I made us some sandwiches, he offered to clean up. Hayley helped him.

He projected an undercurrent of anger, but it diminished some. As they did dishes, I watched as he teased Hayley. They had always been close. They were about fourteen months apart in age. Even though Hayley was the older one, Flynn always acted like her big brother. He kept her safe.

When they laughed about something, I breathed a sigh of relief. Maybe our family would eventually leave the scars of our past behind and start a new, normal life.

During the night, when I heard a noise, I sat up in bed.

"Lilian!" Ike cried out. "Lilian!"

I quietly tiptoed to the door and opened it. Ike cried like a little boy and not like a boy on the cusp of manhood.

"She's in the next room," I whispered.

He hugged me close. "Don't let him take me. I never want to go back there."

Tears streamed down my cheeks as I whispered words of comfort to him. Lilian held a lamp as she waited in her doorway.

"You're safe now, Ike," I whispered. "We'll take care of you. No one will hurt you again."

He loosened his hold on me. "Can I sleep on the floor next to you, Lilian?"

She hesitated. I nodded.

"Of course. Justine will fetch you a blanket," she said as she led him into the room.

I retrieved a throw from the parlor and brought it in. He curled up on the floor, and I gently laid it over him. Lilian climbed into bed and reached down to brush his hair back from his face.

As I returned to my room, I wiped the tears from my eyes. The light dimmed and flickered off as I prayed for my baby brother. He just needed us to love him. I prayed that in time, his broken heart would heal.

CHAPTER 25

May 11, 1893

GRADY

On Thursday, we finally rode out to bring in the Mason Gang. Perry and Xavier arrived on Tuesday. The sheriff and his deputy arrived the next day. On Wednesday, we scouted out the Irving property and devised a plan. Deacon sketched a map from memory.

"There was a wagon here." Deacon pointed to the map. "We can light some dynamite. That will create a distraction. Me and Grady will skirt around to the back of the barn."

Perry nodded. Then he pointed to a spot on the map. "Xavier and I will hide behind this building. None of the guards patrol that area. Best spot to lay down cover fire."

"Jakes and I will move into position here during the explosion." Sheriff Wilkes pointed to a mound on the far side of the property.

I took a shaky breath as I mounted Sunbeam. It was risky. Facing down a gang of outlaws always was. I sure hoped Deacon's idea worked. I wanted it to end that day.

We rode out to where we planned to leave our horses.

Then Deacon belly-crawled toward the wagon. He positioned the dynamite and inched away as he unraveled the long fuse. When he joined us, he lit the fuse.

I held my breath as we waited for the explosion. The seconds ticked by too slowly. Then all at once, a loud bang shook the earth. Smoke and wood splinters filled the air. Deacon and I ran along a nearby wash and made our way behind the barn.

Gunshots erupted. Some from the positions of our men. Shots came from the front of the barn and corral. Deacon kicked in the back barn door.

The sound of a rifle reloading snagged my attention. Victor pointed the weapon between Deacon's shoulder blades.

"Nice try, Colter. I suppose you think we didn't see you sneaking around all week."

My stomach tightened as another man poked a gun barrel into my back. I lowered my pistol as Deacon dropped his.

Then a hard object connected with my head. I crumpled to my knees. My face hit the dirt, and blackness swallowed my vision.

DEACON

"Deacon! Grady!"

Someone called my name in the distance. I shook off the fog and sat up. Grady groaned next to me.

"Deacon! Grady!"

"Over here!" The words came out slightly slurred.

I blinked. Then I helped Grady up.

Perry joined us.

"Thank God. We were worried they took you with them."

"What happened?" I asked.

"We captured Amos Thompson and Caleb Mason."

Grady spat. "Victor? Harper?"

Xavier shook his head.

Grady growled and beat his hand against the wall of the barn.

We had been so close and failed. It was my fault. I didn't think that anyone saw us. I should have been more vigilant.

As I stepped out into the bright sunlight, I squinted. A blood bay lay on its side.

"Deacon," Perry said. "I'm sorry."

Sergeant.

My heart hammered against my rib cage as I ran to my horse. I skidded to a stop and dropped to my knees when I saw the large pool of blood. My eyes burned.

"No. No. No."

I reached out and stroked his stiff neck.

"No!"

His lifeless eyes stared back at me.

"No," I whispered as my lip trembled. Not Sergeant.

I rested my head on his powerful neck as my shoulders shook. "You were such a good horse. I'm sorry."

While I stroked his neck, I repeated the words over and over. He didn't deserve such a brutal death. We had so many good years yet to come. Only they stole the time from us.

"Deacon," Grady whispered my name. "We need to go."

I let him help me to my feet. As we walked away from the horse that had been my companion since I was sixteen,

183

my heart bled. I wasn't ready to say goodbye.

When I glanced over my shoulder, I noticed the deep gash across his neck. They deliberately killed my horse.

As my thoughts retreated inward, I mounted Bear. Sergeant was gone. It was my fault. We failed to capture Victor Mason and Galen Harper. That was my fault, too.

I glanced at Grady. I failed my best friend. He counted on me to come up with the perfect plan. I thought it had been. Only I failed him. I didn't deserve to call myself his friend.

Memories from the school yard came forward. Freak. Weirdo. Idiot. Boys shoved me to the ground. They laughed at me.

Guess they had been right. I was a freak.

For years, I tried to convince myself that my idiosyncrasies kept my gifts in check. My memory was better than most. My observation skills paralleled none. Yet, my odd behavior drew negative attention to me. No one wanted to be my friend. They avoided that freak, Deacon Colter. They were right.

When we arrived at the Cahill's ranch, the sheriff and his deputy pushed on with their prisoners. I offered to care for Grady's horse, but he turned me down.

His hollow expression reminded me I had failed him.

I said nothing during supper. As soon as it was done, I retired to the barn where I laid awake long into the night, replaying each decision, trying to figure out where I went wrong. I came up empty every time.

The next morning, I thanked Aunt Mary for her hospitality. I offered her some money to cover the cost of food, but she refused it. Said she was glad to hear the news from home and to help us.

Xavier and Perry rode ahead of Grady and me. We rode

back to Prescott in silence.

Without thinking, both Grady and I pulled our horses to a stop in front of Lilian's house. No matter how dead I felt inside, I wanted to see her. She would worry if she didn't lay eyes on me. At least I would not fail one person today.

I knocked on the door, and Flynn opened it.

"It's Deacon and Grady," he announced over his shoulder as he stepped back.

He already looked better than a few days ago. Gone were the sunken eyes. A youthful sheen returned to his skin. He filled out some.

Lilian rushed forward and wrapped her arms around me. I hugged her close as I held on to her, my lifeline.

"Deacon, what is it?" My shirt muffled her voice.

I coughed.

"Come, sit out back with me."

She took my hand in hers and led me to a chair. "Tell me what happened."

Then the full story spilled from my lips. How I failed Grady. I failed Sergeant. I failed myself.

She stood behind me and wrapped her arms around my shoulders.

"It's not your fault, Deacon."

I shook my head. "It is."

"No, it's not. Look, you got two of them. I'm grateful they will jail Caleb for a long time."

Her words settled over my heart as she came around and sat on my lap. I held her close to me. Just her presence pulled me from my morose self-recrimination.

"Thank you for all you've done. You sent my brothers to me. You helped capture Caleb. Without your plan, he could still be out there."

"Grady." My voice cracked.

"I'm sure he's disappointed. Frustrated. But, in time, he'll see what a positive milestone today was. It wasn't the result he hoped for, but that doesn't change how meaningful it was."

I sighed and finally looked into her eyes.

"You're a good man, Deacon. Smart. Handsome. Compassionate. Loyal."

She placed her hands on my cheeks. "I love you."

Who was this woman who proclaimed her love for me even after I confessed all my failures?

"I love you," she whispered.

Then she leaned in and kissed me. Sweetly, softly, tenderly. I lost myself to her kiss and returned it with barely restrained longing. I didn't deserve her or her love. But, I accepted it.

At last, I pulled away from her. She slid from my lap and stood.

"I best head home," I said.

"Thanks again, Deacon. For sending my brothers here. Even Shane. I'm sure that took some convincing."

I nodded as I headed back through the house. Grady narrowed his eyes as I walked past him. Then I mounted Bear and headed back home. I heard Grady behind me, though he did not catch up.

———

GRADY

The excitement I felt from Justine's kisses faded the moment Deacon walked back into the house. I said my farewells and followed him out of the Harper's home.

He had a head start. I didn't really feel like talking to him, anyway. He let Victor get away. My best friend failed me.

My anger simmered as I watched him on that stupid brown horse. He was convinced no one knew we were coming and he could not have been more wrong.

When we arrived back at the ranch, I took care of Sunbeam. Then I stormed toward my home. Ellie Mae saw us ride in and tried to corner me. I brushed her off and continued on home.

As I opened the door, I tossed my things in the corner. Deacon stood.

"I'm sorry, Grady."

My rage boiled over. I grabbed his shirt and shoved him backward until his back hit the wall. I yelled in his face.

"You're sorry? You're sorry!"

He extracted himself from my grip. I swung at him. My fist connected with his jaw. He pushed me back. I charged at him and pounded his stomach. Then his face.

When he went to the ground, he refused to defend himself. I continued to strike him.

"You let them get away!"

"I failed you."

The words broke through my rage. I dropped to my knees and yelled at the top of my lungs.

Deacon sat up and watched me.

I slumped forward and pounded my fists on the wood floor. Then the rage faded. Emptiness slithered into my soul, slowly cutting off all feeling in my heart until only numbness remained.

"He got away. Again."

"I know," Deacon said softly as he wiped some blood from his lip.

Doggone it. I beat up my best friend. The one man who always had my back. And I hated myself for it.

"Let's patch you up," I said as I stood.

He pushed himself up before sitting at the table. I cringed at the sight of his face. I nailed him hard. Purple circled his right eye.

I shook my head. He was significantly bigger than me and could have easily knocked me out. Yet he took the brunt of my rage.

"Why do you do that?" I growled at him.

"Do what?"

"Not defend yourself."

He looked away as I handed him a towel wrapped around some ice chips.

"I deserved it."

I sighed as I made some coffee. "No, you didn't. I was out of line."

"I failed you."

"I failed myself, Deacon. It frustrates me that Victor got away. I shouldn't have blamed you."

"But it's my fault."

"No, it isn't. We did the best we could."

I set a cup of steaming coffee in front of him.

"Can you forgive me?" I asked.

He frowned. "Always."

Sometimes I wondered why he did that. Let me off the hook so quickly. He treated me far better than I ever treated him. His messed up face was proof of it.

"Your mama is gonna give me grief for that."

He snorted. "She won't know you did this."

"There you go again."

"What?"

"Why are you always so forgiving towards me? I don't

deserve it. Not after taking my anger out on you."

He sighed. Then he set the towel down. I cringed as he sipped his coffee. A nasty bruise formed under his eye.

"A part of me feels like I deserve it. I let you down."

"But you didn't. That was just my anger speaking."

"The other part of me, the rational part, knows that we've both said and done some things we don't really mean today. We're brothers. Maybe not by birth, but by circumstance. I would want you to forgive me, so I forgive you."

I watched him as he finished his coffee. At length, he said, "Head over to Ellie Mae. She'll want to hear the news, both the good and the bad."

I nodded as I stood and did just that.

CHAPTER 26

DEACON

The next morning was Saturday. I dreaded joining the family for breakfast, knowing the state of my face would upset Mama and probably result in a conversation with Papa in the barn, especially if he noticed Grady's bruised knuckles. Maybe he wouldn't put two and two together.

Grady and I headed over to the big house. As soon as I opened the door, Mama gasped.

"My goodness. Sam, go get my medical bag."

"I'm fine, Mama. It's from yesterday. Nothing to be done about it."

Sam hovered in the doorway. I shook my head. Then he returned to his seat at the table. Grady and I took our usual seats.

"How did that happen?" Papa asked instead of saying grace like I hoped.

When I didn't answer him, he frowned. I would not lie. Nor was I going to tell him what happened between Grady and me. We were men, and it wasn't any of my papa's business.

After a few seconds, Papa bowed his head and blessed

the meal. When he finished, Ellie Mae started passing the plates.

"Grady mentioned you caught two of the rustlers."

I nodded as I ate my breakfast.

Grady told the story to my family. I was fine right up to the point when he mentioned Sergeant. As soon as he said my horse's name, my jaw twitched, and I set down my silverware. I sipped my coffee while I tried to regain control.

"I'm sorry, son," Papa said. He reached over and squeezed my shoulder. "We'll get you a new horse."

"I can pay for it on my own."

"Nonsense," he said. "We'll cover it."

Mama smiled at me. It was useless to argue.

"Bear would be an alright choice," I said. "He's the one Uncle Adam was letting me borrow. Seems the horse likes me."

"Does it hurt?" Vi asked, touching her cheekbone.

"Some. It'll heal."

"I thought we might head into town this afternoon," Grady said. "Get you a new saddle. See how the Harpers are faring."

I nodded.

He told my family about Lilian's brothers and how I paid for their stage fare.

"You did a good thing," Mama said. "Sounds like those boys need love and a safe home."

"Lilian was pretty pleased," I admitted.

When breakfast finished, I lingered at the table. Baby Ashley fussed, so I leaned down and lifted her out of her bassinet.

"Here, let me take her," Ellie Mae said.

I held out my hand for the bottle. "I'd like to feed her."

Ellie Mae smiled. "Alright."

I rocked Ashley in my arms as I fed her. She made me feel human again. Her sweetness and innocence brought me joy. I smiled down at her as she finished eating. Then I placed a towel over my shoulder and burped her before I held her in my arms again. She smiled up at me.

Ellie Mae stood next to me and smiled down at her angel.

"She's the happiest baby I know."

Ellie Mae snorted. "You never had to get up in the middle of the night to feed her."

I laughed and handed her to her mama.

"You'll be a great father one day."

I smiled and headed out to the barn. Papa had just finished talking with Adam.

"Bear is all yours now."

"Thanks Papa."

He followed me as I walked toward Bear's stall.

"You want to talk about what happened?"

I coughed. "About Sergeant? No."

"Between you and Grady?"

"We worked it out."

As I stopped in front of Bear's stall, I saw Papa out of the corner of my eye.

"You sure?"

I nodded. "If you'll excuse me, I need to head into town."

"Would you mind taking your mother and sister in with you?"

I held back a groan. That required the wagon. Of course, if I was buying a new saddle, I needed the wagon anyway, since I couldn't ride with two saddles.

"Yes, sir."

Papa thanked me.

I whistled for Bear to come over. He nudged my arm.

"Sorry, Bear. We'll go for a ride tomorrow."

He snorted.

By the time I hitched the wagon, Mama and Vi waited outside of the barn. Grady was nowhere to be seen.

"Grady said he'd ride in later," Vi said. "If you want to bring your horse, I can drive home."

"Really?"

"Sure. Ellie Mae taught me how."

Mama nodded. "She's quite good now."

"Alright."

I placed a long lead on Bear, but no saddle. Then I tied him to the wagon. He nickered but settled down by the time we reached town.

Mama and Vi hurried to several stores. I untied Bear, tossed the blanket over his back, and headed over to Anderson's Livery. Thomas was one of the best leather workers in town.

"Morning, Deacon," he greeted me.

I greeted him before I explained why I was looking for a new saddle.

"I have one over here. It's like your old one."

"I'm surprised you remember it."

"It was one of my favorite ones to make."

Once I looked it over, I ran a hand along the smooth seat. It would do nicely, so I paid him for it. Then I saddled Bear. After double checking the straps, I hoisted myself up into the new saddle. Bear side stepped at first. Then he calmed.

"Let's take a ride," I whispered to my new horse.

He took off as soon as I squeezed his sides. I let him ride fast out of town on the path to Granite Lake. We only rode far enough for both Bear and me to feel like we had a satisfying run. Then I pointed him back toward town.

When I arrived at the Harper's house, I heard the commotion before I dismounted. I quickly tied Bear to the post. Then I swung the door open.

"Stop it!" Ike screamed.

Shane and Flynn squared off against each other, similar to Grady and me the night before. Flynn took a swing at Shane.

In two strides, I was behind Flynn. I grabbed him around the shoulders, pinning his arms to his side. Then I dragged him over to the dining table. Lilian held out a chair.

"Sit. Down," she commanded. "In *this* house, my house, we don't settle disputes with our fists. We sit and talk it out."

The sharp tone in her voice gave me pause.

Flynn remained standing, so I pressed down on his shoulders until he sat.

"Listen here, young man. This anger you feel like taking out on everyone will get you into trouble, like our father. Is that what you want? To become like the man who neglected us? Who treated us like trash?"

Flynn crossed his arms and frowned.

"Answer me!"

"No ma'am."

Lilian sighed loudly. "Good. Now tell me what this is about."

Shane opened his mouth. I eyed him and he shut up.

"I'm tired of Shane treating me like I'm a kid."

Lilian scoffed. "Swinging at him with your fists isn't very manly now, is it?"

Whatever else was on the tip of Flynn's tongue died as she propped her hands on her hips.

"And you!" She turned toward Shane. I stepped aside.

"You should know better. Is this how you managed disputes after I left?"

Shane shrank back.

"Sorry, Lilian."

"Let's get one thing straight," she said as she made eye contact with each of her brothers. "You start a fight under my roof and you'll be out of this house faster than you can blink."

They stared at the floor.

"Understand?"

"Yes, Lilian," they replied, one at a time.

I hid a smile. She didn't put up with their troublemaking. Good. They needed a firm hand when it was couched in love.

"Now, Shane, I believe you were going to take Hayley to do the shopping."

Her older brother nodded. Hayley scurried around the table before they walked out the door. I closed it behind them.

"You," she said to Flynn, "Need to see about a summer job."

"I ain't going to school in the fall. I'm too old for that."

She glared at him.

An idea came to mind. I cleared my throat. "You know, Sam needs help at the ranch. Flynn already knows some about cattle. Maybe he could hire on as a cowboy."

Lilian glanced at me. "Well, that's the smartest idea I've heard all day. What do you think?"

Flynn uncrossed his arms. "I suppose that'd be okay."

"Good," I said. "Then you can drive my mama and sister back to the ranch when they finish shopping. Go pack your things."

Vi would be disappointed, but it was best to channel the boy's anger into something useful sooner rather than later.

Ike flopped onto the couch.

Lilian smiled at me. "Hello there."

"You know you're a little scary when you're mad."

She laughed. "Kinda necessary to keep three brothers in line."

I pulled her close to me. As I leaned down for a kiss, she placed a hand on my chest and pushed me away.

"Not a chance, mister. Not until you explain what happened to your face. Or did you forget I saw you yesterday after-noon?"

I sighed. "Just a little kiss?"

She rolled her eyes and placed a peck on my cheek. Flynn entered the room.

"Guess it'll have to wait until after I introduce him to my mama and Vi."

I hurried out of the house with Flynn following on my heels. After I introduced Mama and Vi to Flynn, they roped him into carrying their purchases to the wagon.

Since he was on his best behavior, I returned to Lilian's house. She sat at the table and sipped some coffee. She slid a steamy cup toward the seat across from her.

"How are you holding up?" I asked.

Her shoulders slumped. "They've changed a lot in six months. In size and temperament."

"The ranch. It was in disrepair."

"I know. Been like that for a long time."

I shook my head. "How did you manage?"

"By taking it a day at a time. Same way I'm managing this. At least I don't have to worry about Papa showing up. I doubt he would set foot in this town, knowing he's a wanted man."

She sipped her coffee. Then she smiled. "Perfect timing, by the way. I wasn't sure how to separate the two of them without shooting a hole in my ceiling."

I laughed. "You wouldn't?"

"No. Now, what happened to you?"

I told her about the fight with Grady.

She shook her head. "Men. Always settling things the hard way."

"In all fairness, it's the first time, and hopefully only time, we've come to blows."

"Good. I'm going to hold you to it."

She stood and set her cup in the sink.

"You eat lunch yet?"

I shook my head.

"Take me out for lunch. Justine can handle Ike, and I need a break."

I smiled as I stood and offered her my arm.

CHAPTER 27

LILIAN

I leaned into Deacon's side as we stepped onto the front porch. I noticed the brown horse tied to the post. "That yours?"

"His name is Bear."

Then he led me over to the brown gelding.

I smiled and reached out to touch Bear's muzzle. The horse looked at me and I thought he almost smiled when I rubbed his face.

"You take good care of him," I whispered.

"I always do."

I laughed. "I was talking to Bear."

"Oh."

Bear nudged Deacon's shoulder. "Alright, boy."

"He really likes you."

"I think he's partial to the brokenhearted."

"Then he's gonna get along well with me."

Deacon placed his arm around my shoulders and hugged me to his side. "Let's go get that lunch."

His fingers trailed down my arm until they connected with mine. Then we walked to a restaurant. We asked for a secluded seat.

"I'm not sure what to do about Flynn. He needs schooling. I don't think he reads very well."

"He needs some time. I can help him in the evenings. See what he knows."

"You would do that?"

"'Course, Lil. I would do anything for you."

My heart danced.

"Cowboying will be good for him. The men in the bunkhouse will shape him up. It'll give him purpose. Come fall, I think you'll see how good it is for him. We can educate him unconventionally. In a way that works better for him."

"Have you always been so wise?"

He smiled as the server delivered our meal. He clasped my hand and prayed for us and the food.

"How is Shane doing?" he asked.

"I don't know. He's felt responsible for us for so long. He needs a life of his own. Justine and I can take care of Ike. We don't need Shane to do that anymore."

"You know," Deacon said. "When we bring in Victor, I'm gonna quit this job."

"Really?"

"I prefer working as a vet at the stockyards. I took this job to help Grady track down the men who killed his parents. We've done that. Now I want to do what I love."

I took a bite of my sandwich.

"Shane would be a perfect replacement," Deacon said. "Seems smart enough. Got tons of experience with cattle."

"And outlaws."

He inclined his head. Then he ate a bite of his food.

"I will mention it to him soon."

"That leaves Ike," he said.

"He's only fourteen and seems pretty traumatized over whatever happened after I left. He's eager to attend school this Monday and again in the fall."

"A summer job would be good for him, too. Maybe out at the ranch."

I shook my head. "I don't think he's gonna want to leave me."

"What about mucking stalls at the livery?"

"That might be good. It's something he could do after school, too."

"My Uncle Thomas, well he's not really my uncle but we call him that, owns Anderson's Livery. I'm sure he'd be happy for the help."

"Should I talk to him?"

"I can take Ike over there after work on Monday," he offered.

I agreed as I finished my meal. I pushed the plate away and leaned back against the chair. A smile spread across my lips. It almost felt like we were parents.

The thought snagged on my heart. I had no right to think about parenting anyone. Not my brothers. Especially not after I failed to protect my child from its murderous father.

A tear trailed down my cheek.

"What's on your mind, Lil?"

I wiped it away. "Thank you, Deacon. Your advice has been very helpful."

His dark brown eyes scrutinized me, much like he had with the brand wall. I could almost picture him trying to rearrange the broken parts of my heart.

After he paid for the meal, he walked me home. Then he headed back to the ranch. I hoped one day I would gain the courage to tell him about my child.

———

JUSTINE

Late Saturday afternoon, Grady stopped by our house. I was excited to see him and wary about what we might argue about. Ironically, I missed those heavy conversations from the early days of our courtship. At least I knew who he was then.

I held the door open and let him in as he handed me flowers. While he watched me, I took them and placed them in the water.

"Justine. I owe you an apology."

I glanced up as I kept my expression blank.

"I was wrong to get angry with you the last time we spoke. You were just watching out for your brothers. I…"

He came around the table and stood in front of me. Then he took my hands.

"I have been consumed with searching for justice for my parents. To where it blinded me to how I was treating you."

I looked at his hands.

"What happened to your knuckles?"

He cleared his throat. "Deacon and I had a heated discussion."

I frowned and removed my hands from his.

"Look, he was the other person I treated poorly."

I stuffed the last flower in the vase.

"How often do you have heated discussions with people?" I asked.

"Only the once."

My gaze traveled up to his face. He looked sincere enough. "Deacon will confirm this?"

"Don't you trust me?"

I snorted. "I'm not sure I even know you, Grady. I thought we were falling in love. I thought you saw a future with me. Then you abandoned me for months on end with no word."

As I propped my hands on my hips, I continued. "Then you show up with no warning. One moment you're kissing me like I'm the only woman for you. Then next you're storming out of my house threatening…"

I lowered my voice. "Threatening my brothers. Then you come back after capturing Caleb and Amos, acting all smitten again. You're hot and cold."

He glanced down. I waited for him to collect his thoughts.

"You're right. I have been inconsistent with you. For that, I am very sorry."

"I need to know you will not turn into a man like my father. I won't live like that. Never again."

He nodded slowly. "I see how my actions felt that way."

He reached for my hand. Then he tapped the bracelet. "You remember what this says?"

"How can I forget? I read it every morning before I put it on."

"I meant it, Justine. My love for you will never end. I haven't done a good job of showing it. That's my fault, and I'm sorry."

I took a deep breath. I loved Grady. But I needed some time to trust him again.

He released his hold on my hand. "I understand. I need to prove it to you."

Tears burned my eyes as I nodded.

"Alright. Give me time. I will do my best to earn your trust again."

My throat constricted as I walked to the door and held it open. After Grady left, I closed it. When second thoughts flooded my heart, I looked out the window and watched him ride away. I hoped he would be true to his word.

CHAPTER 28

JUSTINE

On Monday morning, I started late at the dry goods store so I could meet with the teacher. Ike and I walked to the school together.

"I hope I make friends," Ike said. "I've never had a friend."

I frowned before I quickly wiped it away. I suppose I never had a friend, either. Just my sisters.

We arrived before the other students. The teacher asked Ike to sit in the back of the classroom so we could speak in private.

"Miss Harper, do you know much about your brother's schooling?"

"We didn't get to attend school much back home. My mama taught us older kids. Then my older sister, Lilian, taught us the basics."

"I'll spend some time with him this morning to assess his grade level. I'll be ready to share my plan this afternoon if you or Lilian could stop by."

"Thank you, Ms. Fletcher."

"Ike," she called him forward. "Before the other students

arrive, let's work on some exercises."

"Yes, ma'am."

After I left, I walked to the livestock inspection office and gave Lilian an update. I told her I would meet with the teacher after school. Then I went to work.

When my shift ended for the day, I walked back to the school.

"What do you think?" I asked Ms. Fletcher.

"Well, his reading level is below his age group, but I think we can overcome that. He knows the basics of math. Again, at a lower level than his age group."

My shoulders slumped. Lilian and I wanted him to get a solid education. It disappointed me he was so far behind.

"Not to worry," Ms. Fletcher said. "If you are open to it, I can spend a few hours every day over the summer teaching him. That way, by the time school starts this fall, and if he works hard, he will start at the same level as the other children his age."

"Oh, thank you, Ms. Fletcher. If there's anything Lilian or I can do to help him, please let us know."

Ms. Fletcher smiled. "He seemed keen to learn in class today, so I am fully confident that he will do well."

As I walked away from school, my steps felt a little lighter. Ike wasn't too far behind. Nothing that some hard work couldn't overcome.

When I stepped onto the boardwalk, a man in all black drew my attention. I stopped and watched as Victor Mason argued with Bart. Then he thrust some paperwork into Bart's hands. Bart gestured wildly before storming off.

Victor looked up and saw me. I froze.

Then he ran toward me. I lifted my skirts and ran toward the boardwalk. I tried to find a public place. As I almost cleared the alleyway, his brawny arms grabbed me from behind.

"Justine Harper."

Victor's hot breath warmed my neck. I swallowed down the bile that rose in my throat. I squirmed, but nothing I did loosened his hold.

"Let me go!"

His hand clamped down over my mouth.

"You always turn up in the wrong place at the wrong time."

I continued to fight against his grip as he dragged me down the alley and through the back streets.

"Justine?"

I closed my eyes at the sound of my father's voice.

"She saw me. With Bart."

As Victor released his hand from my mouth, my father slapped me hard across the face.

"Stupid girl."

"Papa," I whined, hoping it might stir some compassion in his stony heart.

"Shut up!" he hissed at me. Then he handed Victor a bandanna. "Gag her."

Victor tied the cloth around my head so tight it pulled against the corners of my mouth. Then he tied my hands behind my back. He tossed me in the back of a wagon and tied my feet together before he threw a tarp over me.

"Be quiet," he growled.

The wagon lurched and rocked. The sounds of the town faded after several minutes. Then the wagon leaned forward at a steep angle. He was taking me back to Harper Ranch.

My stomach tightened. I started making noise. I sat up and pulled the tarp off me before I leaned over the edge of the wagon.

"Go ahead, stupid girl. Leap over the side of the mountain. You'll save me the trouble of getting rid of you." Papa's sinister words troubled me.

I peered over the edge and sure enough, I would have leapt to my death. I plopped down and leaned back against the wagon.

Then I prayed. *Please, Lord, let someone notice I'm gone. Help them find me.*

————

LILIAN

Towards the end of the workday, Deacon left before me to take Ike over to his uncle's livery.

When I arrived home from work, Justine wasn't there, but Deacon and Ike were. I waited a few minutes until Hayley ushered me and Deacon out of the house for our dinner date.

"You deserve a night out. I'll make supper for the rest of us."

I reluctantly allowed Deacon to take me to dinner. Our conversation stilted as I was distracted. It wasn't like Justine to shirk her responsibility.

"Do you think she ran into Grady on her way home?" I asked him.

"Not likely. He went straight to the ranch, as far as I know."

When he walked me home, I invited him in for a few minutes.

"Justine?" I called out.

"She's still not home," Hayley said.

I glanced at the clock. Seven.

Someone knocked on the door. Deacon turned and opened it. A boy thrust a piece of paper at him and ran off.

He handed it to me.

I unfolded it, and my heart sank to the floor. Then I handed it back to Deacon as I slid onto the nearest chair.

He read it aloud. "Grady for Justine. You have three days to show up at her home. Victor."

"What do we do?" I asked.

"I'm gonna get the sheriff and Perry. We'll figure this out."

Shane, Hayley, and Ike all looked at me. I put coffee on, as I did not know what else to do.

Shane jerked the door open. "I'm gonna help get her back. No one knows the ranch like I do."

"Be careful."

He nodded before he left.

For the first time in a year, I prayed. I don't know when I let go of my grudge against God. It happened slowly. So, I turned to Him, and I prayed for Justine's safety. That Victor would not hurt her. I prayed for the safety of the men in my life and that they'd return with Justine unharmed.

CHAPTER 29

DEACON

I smoothed out the paper and handed it to the sheriff. "He took Justine to Harper Ranch."

Victor wanted Grady. I shook my head. I would not let Grady trade himself for Justine. Victor would certainly put a bullet in his head. And Grady cared enough for her to sacrifice himself. My plan involved keeping them both alive.

I paced the length of the sheriff's office until Perry joined us. I needed to think. There must be a way to rescue Justine without giving up Grady.

"Lilian said that Victor took Justine," Shane said as he entered the sheriff's office. "I'm here to help."

"You should go home, Shane."

He locked his eyes on mine. "She's my sister. It's the only home I've known for twenty-six years. No one knows it like I do."

The sheriff asked Shane to draw a map of the entire property. Thirty minutes later, Grady and Xavier arrived.

Grady's stoic expression concerned me. I was certain he would risk his own life to save Justine. I thought we might get her back with no one losing their life.

"At first light, we'll ride down there," the sheriff said. "We stop at the Cahill's and rest and water the horses. Our best bet is to arrive at the ranch just before dusk. The light from lanterns will help us figure out where they are on the ranch."

"I don't know. They know their land and buildings better than we do," I said. "Darkness may work to their advantage."

"You're right," Perry said. "Daylight is our best option."

"They'll keep her in the hideout room," Shane said. "They never go into the house, so I doubt they would this time."

"We should search the house first, just to be sure," Xavier said. "They may change their behavior if they think you're helping us."

Shane frowned. "They would have more cover and an easier escape from the barn."

It was late by the time we finished planning. Grady, Shane, and I spent the night at the Harper's house. Grady and I slept in the parlor.

The next morning, we rode out, prepared to be gone for days if needed. I kissed Lilian goodbye and promised again to bring her sister back.

We said little until we arrived at the Cahill's ranch. We stayed overnight there and rode out to Harper's at first light.

When Wednesday morning dawned, I ate very little for breakfast. My stomach churned. I would not let Grady down again. Our plan was solid, but there were so many unknowns.

Once we arrived at Harper Ranch, Shane rode to the barn according to the plan while Xavier sneaked into the house. When he gave the all-clear, Shane dismounted his horse.

"Papa! I'm here to help!"

Galen Harper appeared in the shadow of the barn doorway. He scanned the area, then grabbed Shane by the neck and dragged him into the shadows.

I inched my way along the outside of the barn as I heard Galen's fist connect with Shane.

"Stupid boy. Where you been? You know I don't like you leaving the property."

"Sorry," Shane groaned. "I was hunting."

"Where are your brothers?"

"In the house," Shane lied.

I peeked through the slats of the barn wall. Galen smacked Shane on the face, splitting his lip. I flinched.

"Lies. We already checked the house."

"They are where you can't hurt them," Justine said.

She was in the corner of the room.

"Shut up, girl!" Galen hollered.

I still didn't locate Victor.

Just then, Grady entered the barn. My stomach dropped to the floor. That was not part of the plan.

"Leave her alone!" Grady yelled.

I motioned for the rest of the posse to surround the barn, and I ran inside after my foolish best friend.

———

GRADY

When I entered the barn, my eyes scanned the room quickly. They had tied up Justine, and she sat in a chair in a back corner of the room. Victor stood over Shane, ready to kick him. Galen Harper stalked toward Justine after her outburst.

"Leave her alone!"

Galen spun around at the sound of my voice. He yanked Justine to her feet and used her as a shield. I couldn't get a clean shot on him, so I aimed at Victor's chest.

"Grady, don't do it."

Deacon's voice came from behind me. "We need to bring him in alive to get the justice you want."

Galen inched closer to the back door of the barn, holding my woman tight against him.

Victor leveled his pistol at my chest, ignoring Shane on the floor.

"Thatcher. We meet at last."

"Drop your weapon, Victor," I said, as Deacon slowly moved closer to Galen and Justine.

"Or what? You'll shoot me? You don't have it in you."

Victor laughed. "I still remember your pretty mama. If we hadn't been in such a hurry, I planned to have a little fun with her."

My shoulders tensed. I jerked forward.

"You move an inch and you're a dead man," Victor said as he backed towards Galen's position and his escape.

Shane crawled along the floor, keeping pace with Victor, but moving ever closer to his father's feet.

I glanced at Deacon. He gave me one sharp nod to let me know he noticed Shane, too. I sure hoped he knew what he was doing.

"And your pa," Victor went on. "He didn't put up a fight. Simpering fool. It was my pleasure to put a bullet in his head."

My stomach churned as the evil man spoke vitriol about my parents. I subtly shuffled forward, keeping my pistol aimed at Victor's chest.

All the sudden, Shane grabbed Justine and pulled her to the ground. He covered her with his body. Victor's gaze darted to them. I lowered my aim to his knee and pulled the trigger. His gun went off as he fell to the ground, but the bullet missed everyone. Deacon hurried forward and kicked Victor's gun away from his grasp.

Galen Harper slipped out the door. Xavier hauled him back into the room and disarmed him. Justine crawled away from her father. Shane sat up and began untying the ropes from Justine's hands and feet.

When she stood to her feet, I ignored everyone else. I ran to her and pulled her close to my chest. Her tears wet my shirt as I stroked her hair.

"It's over," I whispered to her. "You're safe."

She pulled back slightly. "Are you alright?"

I nodded.

"But you're bleeding."

I followed her gaze to my gut. When the shock wore off, I doubled over in pain as I fell to the floor.

CHAPTER 30

JUSTINE

"Grady!"

I screamed his name as he collapsed on the floor.

"Help me. Please help!" I cried out.

The sheriff entered the barn and cuffed Victor as I cried over Grady's still body. His deputy led my father away, with Perry and Xavier guarding them both.

"Please, Deacon."

He hurried to my side. Then he turned Grady over. "Bullet went clean through."

Deacon tore off his shirt and pressed it into the wound. "Here, press as hard as you can."

Then he took his knife and popped off the end of one of his bullets. He lifted the blood-soaked shirt and poured the black powder from the bullet over the wound. Then he lit a match.

"Step back."

I did right as he touched the match to the powder. Grady's body lurched, and he howled before losing consciousness again.

When Deacon turned him over, he pried off the top of

another bullet. I looked away. Grady regained consciousness long enough to scream out before he slipped under again.

"He needs a doctor," Deacon said. "I only bought him some time."

"Congress has a doctor," Shane said. "He's gonna be the closest."

"Help me get him up into a wagon."

"You got this, Deacon?" Perry asked. "We want to take these two in."

"You go. Shane and Justine can help me."

Perry nodded and left.

My tears slowed. I sat in the back of the wagon with Grady as Shane drove us to Congress. Deacon followed behind on his horse. He had tied Shane and Grady's horses to the back of the wagon.

As the wagon hit a bump, I yelled at my brother.

"Be careful!"

Then I whispered to Grady, praying he could hear me. "Stay with me. Hold on. We're getting you help."

A sob wrangled free from my throat. "Please don't leave me. I love you."

By the time Shane stopped in front of the doctor's office, Grady looked very pale and weak. Deacon slung him over his shoulder and took him into the doctor's office. I clung to Shane as he helped me to a chair in the waiting room.

"I want to be with him."

"Sit. Let the doctor work."

He sat beside me and I leaned into my big brother's side as I whispered prayers for my beloved's life.

———

DEACON

As soon as I deposited Grady onto an exam table, the doctor's nurse shoved me out of the room. Then I joined Shane and Justine in the waiting room. I pinched the bridge of my nose, hoping to stem the tears that came to the surface.

My best friend was dying.

I swallowed the lump in my throat. I did the best I could to buy him time, but if he had internal bleeding…

I refused to allow the thought to take root. God was in the business of doing miracles. So that's what I asked for. A miracle. Healing for Grady. Skill for the doctor and his nurse.

One hour passed. Then two.

I tried not to lose hope.

Finally, the doctor came out.

"We opened the bullet wound and pulled out a few fragments that remained. Nothing major was damaged. We stopped the bleeding and cauterized the wound again."

He stood in front of me.

"Never seen someone do what you did. It may have saved his life."

I let out the breath I had been holding before I stumbled back into the chair.

"He lost a lot of blood, so it's going to be a few days before you can transport him home."

Justine thanked the doctor and thanked me. "Can I see him now?"

"Not yet," the doctor said. "He's resting. Why don't you come back tomorrow?"

"We can stay at Aunt Mary's house," I suggested.

Shane rode back to Prescott that day. I tied my horse and Grady's behind the wagon. Then Justine rode with me in the wagon to Cahill Ranch.

When we arrived, Aunt Mary took good care of Justine, coaxing her to eat and drink. Then she fixed up the guest room for her.

The next morning, I joined the Cahills for breakfast.

"I think we should wait until this afternoon to go visit him," I said.

Justine frowned. "When he wakes up, I want to be with him."

"That isn't likely until this afternoon."

"Fine."

"Uncle Warren, can I help around the place while I'm here?"

He considered it and gave me a list of things that needed fixed up. Then he showed me where he stored his tools.

I was thankful for the distraction while I waited for the hours to roll by.

Finally, after lunch, I saddled my horse and a horse for Justine. Then we went into town to visit Grady.

"He just woke up," the nurse said.

Justine's breath caught when she saw him. His skin looked ashen. His eyes fluttered open, and he still managed a suave smile for her. I hovered in the doorway to give them some privacy.

"You alright?" his voice was weak.

"Yeah. You're the only one with a scratch."

He chuckled, then groaned. "Doc says it's a little more than a scratch."

She brushed his hair back from his forehead.

"Where's Deacon?"

"I'm here."

I sat in the chair on the other side of the bed.

He placed his hand on Justine's cheek. "Give us a minute?"

After she left the room, he turned to me. "Thank you."

Coughs wracked his body. When they subsided, he continued. "For helping bring them in. For saving Justine. For saving me."

"I'd say anytime, but frankly, I hope to never be in that position again."

He held my gaze. "All the same. Thanks."

I squeezed his shoulder and stood.

"Be sure Ellie Mae knows I'm alright."

"I'll send a telegram before I head back to the Cahills. We'll be staying there until you're well enough to go home."

I sent Justine back in. After an hour, she was ready to return to the Cahills.

"He fell asleep pretty quickly," she said. "I was hoping he'd wake again, but I suppose I should just let him rest."

We continued the routine for the next week and a half. On June first, the doctor said Grady could travel home to the ranch.

The morning of June second, I hitched the Harper's horse to the wagon and tied my horse and Grady's horse behind it. I thanked the Cahills for their hospitality again. At least with all the repairs I completed, I felt like I gave them something in return.

Then I helped Justine up to the wagon seat before I joined her and drove to the doctor's office. I laid out the horse's blankets as a cushion and Grady's saddle as a pillow. Then I helped him into the wagon. Once he was settled, we headed for home.

In Prescott, I dropped Justine off and asked her to tell

Lilian I would see her on Sunday. Then I drove Grady back to Colter Ranch.

When Ellie Mae saw us coming down the lane, she hurried out of the house to greet. She motioned for me to stop at her house.

"What are you doing?" Grady groused.

"You're going to stay with me until you're better," Ellie Mae said.

"I want to stay in my room in my house."

"Stop being so stubborn."

I smiled as they argued, knowing who was going to win it.

"I've already prepared a room for you. Deacon, can you help him upstairs?"

"I can walk upstairs on my own."

I looped my arm around his waist as he placed his around my shoulders. Despite his claims that he didn't need help, I was glad I did. He was winded by the time we got him into bed.

"You listen to your sister, you hear?" I warned him before I left.

After I finished caring for the horses, with Uncle Adam's help, I went home. I made some coffee and sat at the table in the silence.

A knock sounded on the door.

"Deacon," Mama greeted me as she pushed the door open. I stood and gave her a big hug. "I heard the commotion and saw you were home. Am I interrupting anything?"

"No, come on in. You want some coffee?"

She nodded. "Grab two plates. I have some fresh apple pie."

"Mmm." I loved my mama. She always knew my favorite.

"I'm so glad you're home," she said as she took a seat and dished up pie for each of us.

"Ellie Mae gave us updates about Grady. We assumed you were alright since you were sending the messages, but it's good to see you again."

"You and Vi cleaned up in here, didn't you?"

"Of course. We didn't want you to come home to a dusty house."

"Thanks, Mama."

For the next hour, I told Mama everything that had happened in the last few weeks. She listened and offered me a second piece of pie. I took one for later.

Towards the end of the conversation, she asked me, "What is next for you? Will you keep working at the livestock inspection office?"

"No. I'm gonna give Perry my notice on Monday if Derek still needs a vet at the stockyards."

"Your papa said when Sam went in last week, he still hadn't replaced you."

I nodded.

"And what about Lilian?"

I smiled. "I'm planning on bringing the Harpers out on Sunday for supper. Remind me to let Ellie Mae know."

Mama laughed. "We already figured that."

She ate a bite of pie before she asked, "Are you going to marry her?"

"I think so. I want to court her. She needs some time. Especially after all the changes in the last few months, taking care of her brothers and all."

I frowned and debated if I should continue. "One of the Mason boys hurt her real bad. So she needs me to take it slow."

"I understand. It's good of you to realize that." She

glanced at the clock. "I better go help Ellie Mae with supper."

When I walked her to the door, she kissed me on the cheek. "Glad you're home and safe."

CHAPTER 31

GRADY

Around the middle of June, I finally felt almost normal again. On the third Sunday of June, I attended church for the first time since the shooting. When Justine arrived, she smiled at me. Then she scolded me.

"Are you sure you're well enough to be out?"

"I'm more than ready. I moved back into my house mid-week. Ellie Mae was driving me crazy."

"Hey, I heard that," she said from behind me.

I took a seat next to Justine. Shane, Flynn, and Ike sat next to Hayley, who sat next to Lilian and Deacon. I smiled. We filled a pew nicely.

During worship, I sang softly, as my gut still ached when I took too deep of a breath. It felt good to see friends, family, and Justine. My parents' murderers were in jail, awaiting trial. Life was good and about to get a lot better that afternoon, or so I hoped.

As soon as the service was over, Shane loaded the Harpers into their wagon. I rode Sunbeam, much to Justine and Ellie Mae's dismay. He needed the exercise as much as I did.

Once we arrived at the ranch, Deacon took my horse

from me. "Ike said he wants to take care of your horse for you."

I sighed. Somehow, I figured Deacon roped him into it.

When I tried to help Justine down from the wagon, she wagged her finger at me. "Don't hurt yourself."

Surely any day the women in my life would stop babying me.

When her feet were on the ground, I laced my fingers with hers and pulled her toward the path along the lake.

"What are you doing?" she asked.

"Walk with me for a spell."

I set a slow pace, hoping to keep any more scolding at bay. Ellie Mae agreed to hold dinner for me when I told her about my plans. Still, I didn't want to keep the family waiting too long.

When we arrived at the spot where she told me all those months ago she wanted to be treated like a princess, I faced her.

"Justine," I started as I clasped her hands. "I hope you have seen my heart over the past few weeks. It was a mistake to choose my desire for justice over you, and I'm sorry."

"Grady, I've already forgiven you for that."

"You have?"

"When you took a bullet to rescue me, I realized you loved me as much as you claimed. You came and rescued me."

I cupped her face in my hand. Then I cleared my throat.

"You're distracting me," I said.

Then I dropped to one knee. Her breath caught.

"We stood in this very spot months ago. You told me you wanted to be treated like a princess and you wanted a godly man. I hope that I have proven to you I am that, despite my failures."

Her eyes brimmed with tears.

"Justine, I love you with all my heart. Will you marry me?"

I held my mother's ring at the tip of her finger as I waited for her reply.

———

JUSTINE

My breath lodged in my throat as Grady asked me to be his wife. Tears burned my eyes as I looked down into his brown-sugar eyes. The fears I had about him before the kidnapping disappeared. I understood his heart. I found my godly man, and his mistakes did not change my feelings for him or his for me.

He cleared his throat, and I realized I was taking too long to answer.

"Yes. Yes, Grady, I want to be your wife."

He slid the ring onto my finger. Then he stood and pulled me tight against him as his lips pressed against mine. When I parted mine, he deepened the kiss as his hands roamed over my back. Fire ignited in my heart as I rested my hands behind his neck and savored his nearness.

After what seemed like forever, he slowed the kiss and ended it. Then he smiled at me, as his eyes reddened. "That's my mother's ring."

"Oh, Grady. I feel so honored."

He coughed, something I learned he did to mask his emotion. Then he slid his hand down my arm and laced his fingers with mine.

"We should go. Ellie Mae won't hold supper for us much longer."

As joy filled my heart, I walked beside the man who would soon become my husband.

Supper sat on the table by the time we entered. We quickly took our seats. Ellie Mae smiled at me before she bowed her head for the blessing.

As soon as Will Colter closed the prayer, the table buzzed with conversation.

"So you said yes," Ellie Mae said.

"Of course."

"Oh, let us see!" Hayley exclaimed.

I held my hand where my sisters could see the ring better.

"It's lovely," Lilian said, though her voice sounded strained.

I knew she was happy for me, but I wondered what bothered her about the news. I made a mental note to ask about it later.

Deacon looked a little sad, too.

"When is the wedding?" Vi asked.

"I thought maybe the second Saturday in September," Grady said. He angled to look at me. "That gives us time to find a house and work through any logistics with your family."

I nodded slowly. "That sounds good."

"Will you have the wedding here?" Hannah asked.

"I want to marry in the church," I said.

"I agree," Grady said. "Especially since we want to live in town, it would be nice to have it at the church. But thank you for the offer."

Hannah smiled. "It is your special day, so whatever you want will be just wonderful."

I appreciated her understanding. I knew how much Grady loved the Colters. Even though she wasn't his mother, I was certain she had filled that void for him.

Throughout the meal, the women asked more questions about what I wanted. They offered help with preparations for the wedding and setting up a home. I felt so loved.

After supper finished, Grady looked worn out. We sat on the couch. I sat on the end with his head resting on a pillow on my lap. Within seconds, he fell asleep.

"Don't let him push himself too hard," I warned Deacon.

"He needs another week before going back to work."

After Lilian finished helping with the dishes, she stared out the window. Deacon noticed too and escorted her outside for a private conversation before I could ask what troubled her.

When they returned, she was smiling and happy again.

I nudged Grady. "Grady."

"Hmm?"

"We need to head home."

He yawned and stretched out. "What time is it?"

"Five o'clock."

"Oh, I'm sorry. I must have dozed off."

He stood and walked me to the barn. We stole a few kisses while Shane hooked up the wagon. When Grady promised to come into town on Friday to look at houses, I asked how we could afford a house.

"With the money I saved from the sale the farm." He tapped his finger on my nose. "The future Mrs. Thatcher can have as nice of a house as she wants."

I grinned. "The future Mrs. Thatcher was thinking about four bedrooms and a large kitchen."

"I think we can arrange that."

He let Shane help me into the wagon. Then I waved to

him as we pulled away.

As soon as we crested the hill, I turned my attention to Lilian.

"What was troubling you earlier?" I asked.

"Oh, nothing."

"No, something was definitely bothering you."

"I'm thrilled for you, Justine. This is your dream, what you've always wanted."

Since she didn't want to tell me, I let it go. Hayley peppered me with a million questions for the rest of the ride home.

CHAPTER 32

LILIAN

A few weeks after Justine and Grady's engagement, the town came alive for the Independence Day Celebration. Try as I might, I didn't feel the excitement.

I missed working with Deacon. He took the job at the stockyards. Our new routine included lunch on Wednesdays, dinner out on Fridays, and Sunday supper at the ranch, or occasionally at my house. I should have been satisfied with that. We were courting, and three times a week was a nice routine.

As I placed my straw hat on my head, I sighed.

"Ike, Hayley, Shane! You ready?"

Ike skidded into the room. "I am."

Shane stood from his seat in the parlor. He plopped his hat on his head.

"Almost!" Hayley called from her room. Then she rushed into the parlor.

"Let's go. I don't want to miss the baseball game," I said.

I ushered my family out the door. Justine waved to us when we arrived. I was glad she saved us seats. Apparently, the game was a bigger draw than I realized.

Deacon smiled when he saw me. He caught the ball Sam threw his direction. Then he threw it to Grady at home plate. The family ganged up on Grady and restricted him to home plate duty. No one was ready for him to run around much, except maybe him.

The game lasted an hour and a half and was full of drama. In the end, the Colter Cowboys won for the third year in a row.

Deacon rushed over to me. He wiped his shirtsleeve across his forehead. Then he leaned down and planted a big kiss on my lips.

"Congratulations," I said.

"So, what shall we do first?"

"Shane, you keep track of Ike?"

He nodded.

Deacon laughed. "You will be an amazing mother. In fact, you already are."

The comment hit a raw spot in my heart. Tears sprang to my eyes. Then a sob choked my throat. Before I knew it, I bawled, right there next to the baseball field.

Deacon placed his hand at the small of my back and guided me to a bench away from the throng of people.

"Lil, what's wrong?"

I hiccupped. "I'm a terrible mother."

He frowned. "I see you with your siblings. You're great. They would be lost without you. You make sure someone is watching out for Ike. You care deeply for them."

"You don't understand."

I turned my eyes on him.

"My baby died because I'm such a terrible mother."

———

DEACON

Lilian's words crashed into my heart.

Baby?

I cleared my throat. Then I took a deep breath.

"What baby?" I asked, afraid of the answer.

She sniffed. Then she looked down at her hands.

"Lil?"

"I… You already know what Caleb did to me."

I placed my arm around her shoulders and rubbed a hand on her arm.

"What I didn't tell you—couldn't tell you—was that one of those times… I ended up pregnant."

My heart ached for her. I could not imagine the horror she faced. Then to end up with child. My poor Lil.

"When I started to show, he became furious. He blamed me for getting pregnant."

She turned wild eyes on me. "He blamed me!"

I tried to keep my features calm and comforting despite the turmoil boiling inside of me. I rubbed my thumb on my finger. As soon as I realized it, I stuffed it in my pocket.

"I failed to protect my baby."

She looked away.

"He beat me. He knocked me to the ground. Then he…"

Her voice broke, and the tears streamed down her face.

"He kicked my womb until I lost my child."

She turned her face into my chest and sobbed. Tears rolled down my cheeks, too. My heart hurt with hers as I stroked her hair and let her cry her heart out.

My sweet Lil.

Oh, how I wished I could roll back the clock. That I

could have met her years ago and protected her from such pain and misery.

"I... I'll understand if you don't want to keep courting me."

I straightened. Then I lifted her face so I could look into her eyes.

"What Caleb did to you was... Horrible. But none of it changes how I feel about you, Lil. I love you."

Her eyes searched mine. I hoped she saw the truth there.

"The only way this courtship will end is with an engagement, when the time is right."

"You want to marry me?"

Her eyebrows drew together as she sat up.

"I just told you I let him murder my child."

"Yes, I heard you heap that guilt on yourself. The way I see it, he abused you. Then he became so violent against you he caused your body to miscarry. None of that is your fault. It's his and his alone. One day he will stand before God and he will pay for it."

I let out a long breath.

"But you, Lil, did nothing wrong. That you became attached to your unborn child is proof of what a wonderful mother you are. You cared for the child regardless of how he came to be."

She blinked. "I never thought of it that way."

"And look what you've done for your sisters, Ike, Flynn, and Shane. They all adore you and need you. No one respects you more than them. They listen to you. It's because of all the years you acted as their mother. It's a testament to what a wonderful mother you are right now. To them."

Lilian wiped her eyes dry.

"And I can't wait to see you in action with our children one day. If we have boys, you won't put up with their nonsense, just like you don't with your brothers. If we have daughters, you will nurture them and help them become compassionate, wonderful young women like your sisters."

"You still want me?"

I closed my eyes. I wanted her more than anything. If only I could help her understand that.

"Lil, I want you to be my wife. My heart is ready now. But yours isn't there yet. And that's alright with me. I can be patient because my greatest desire is to show you love. Love is kind and patient. It gives. So, I'm not formally asking you right now. I will know when the time is right. Trust me."

She rested her head against my chest. I don't know how long we sat there. I waited until she composed herself.

She finally pulled back and smiled at me. "You should change out of that uniform."

I laughed. "Happy to."

We walked hand in hand back to her home. She waited outside as I changed. Then we went back to the Independence Day Celebration. I played some games to win her a trinket. She laughed with me as we ran the three-legged race. We ate a picnic lunch with her brothers and sisters.

I couldn't remember seeing her smile so much. I loved her and longed for the day when her heart healed more. Every day, I prayed for it.

CHAPTER 33

August 14, 1893

GRADY

By the middle of August, Justine and I purchased a house. We furnished it and I tried to wait patiently for our wedding day. I had already moved into it, much to Deacon's chagrin.

On Monday, I sat in the courtroom for the start of the trial against Victor Mason. Galen Harper, Caleb Mason, and Amos Thompson had already been sentenced for rustling since there was no evidence against them for murder.

They had questioned Bart Mason for his involvement with the gang, based on the conversation Justine had witnessed. There was not enough evidence for legal action against him, though he lost his job at the stockyards.

Victor murdered my parents. I saw it all, and I was ready to declare it publicly.

My attorney, Mel Glassman, squeezed my hand before I entered the courtroom. "Remember what we prepared. Stick to the facts. If you get emotional, take a deep breath. Then continue on. It's alright if you show some emotion."

I nodded.

I looked around the courtroom. Justine waved when she saw me. Then she slid into the seat next to me. Ellie Mae sat on my other side.

My heart raced as I listened to the testimony against Victor Mason. Former Sheriff Sloane testified about his investigation. Several other eyewitnesses testified about Victor's involvement.

"The prosecution calls Grady Thatcher to the stand."

As my heart slammed against my chest, I coughed before I stood and walked toward the stand. I swore to tell the truth. Then I sat down in the witness box.

Victor narrowed his eyes at me.

It was all I needed to find my courage again. I was no longer a scared teenager watching him kill my parents. I was a man. We hunted for him; and by God's grace, we brought him in. Now it was my turn to tell my story.

"On the day in question, tell me where were you?" the District Attorney asked.

"I was at my family's farm working in the barn."

"And what did you see?"

"I heard a gunshot, so I peered out the barn door. I saw…" I coughed. "My father's plow horses ran out of control, dragging him behind."

"Did you see who fired the gun?"

"Not that time."

"What else happened?"

"I saw a man in all black dismount from a horse. He ran toward my mother, only a few feet from where I stood. He placed the barrel of his pistol against her head."

Ellie Mae gasped. I kept my gaze on the prosecutor, as I knew I could not complete my testimony if I looked at her.

"He pulled the trigger and my mother's lifeless body fell

to the ground."

"Did you get a clear view of the man?"

"Yes. I was close enough to see his face."

"And do you see that man in the courtroom?"

"Yes, sir. It was Victor Mason."

"What happened next?"

"I stepped back into the barn out of sight. Then I waited until the four men rode off. When I thought it was safe to come out, I ran to my mother first, even though I knew she could not survive the point-blank shot."

I coughed again. Then I took a deep breath.

"I checked on my father. He was dead. Shot through the heart."

The defense council asked me a few questions. Mel had prepared me for them, so I reiterated my testimony. Then they excused me.

I took my seat in the gallery between Justine and Ellie Mae.

The trial took over a week. I sat through every word of the testimony. Besides my parents, Victor Mason also murdered four other people, at least that witnesses saw. They found him guilty and sentenced him to death.

When they read the verdict, I hugged Ellie Mae for a long moment. We finally received justice for my parents.

The prosecutor told us we could witness Victor's hanging. I had no desire to see such a thing. Ellie Mae declined as well. Knowing his sentence was enough for us.

The evening after the sentencing, Deacon stopped by.

"How are you?" he asked.

I puffed my cheeks and blew out a breath. "Alright."

"Let's go get some supper," he suggested.

I walked with him to a nearby restaurant. While we waited for our food to arrive, I told him about the trial.

"We waited so long for justice. It seems so strange that it's finally over."

"Are you going to keep working at the livestock inspection office?"

"Yes. I like the work. Plus, I'm training Shane. Justine would never forgive me if I left her brother without someone to watch his back."

Deacon laughed. "I'm glad you like it."

"Hey, I…" I picked at the food on my plate. "Thank you. Thanks for working there and helping me track down the Mason Gang."

He reached across the table and squeezed my shoulder. "You would do the same for me."

He was right.

"How are you doing?" I asked him.

"Alright, I suppose. It's weird going home to an empty house."

I felt a little guilty. "I should have waited to move out."

"Oh, no. I'm glad you are moving on."

I snorted. "Couldn't wait to get rid of me?"

"You know that's not what I meant."

I grinned.

"I am happy you found a good woman. You are preparing for the life I'm sure your parents always hoped for."

I took a sip of iced tea to hide the emotion stirring.

"You and me, we will always be friends. We should keep meeting regularly."

"Deacon, you're right. We should. Just because our lives are changing doesn't mean we stop being brothers."

"Exactly."

"So, you were saying the house is too quiet?"

"Yeah. I spend a little time every evening working with Flynn. Teaching him how to read better. I like to teach him math without him realizing it. Of course, I teach him about God and how to be a man who doesn't settle his disputes with his fists, but with his wits instead."

I smiled.

"What?"

"You will be an excellent father. You and Lilian already have parenting figured out. And you aren't even married yet."

He frowned and glanced away.

"Is everything alright between you?"

"Yeah. With you getting married, it makes me long for marriage, too."

"So ask her."

"She's not quite ready yet."

I raised an eyebrow. "How do you know?"

"I just do. Not unlike I knew this last week was hard for you."

"Alright. I'll stop pestering you. Maybe when the two of you stand for us, it'll set her mind in that direction."

"We'll see."

When I walked home after supper, I wondered about what kept Deacon from proposing. I thought it might not be as obvious as he made it sound. Perhaps he was afraid she might say no, even though she never would.

———

DEACON

As I rode home after having supper with Grady, I considered his words. How did I know Lilian wasn't ready for me to propose? Even when I said it, I wasn't so sure.

Every time I left Lilian on Wednesday and Friday, it was harder and harder to leave. To go home to an empty house. An empty house where I spent more time than I would ever admit, dreaming of her there.

When I was with her, we talked around it. We shared how things were going with our jobs. She updated me about her siblings. I told her about my progress with Flynn. I told her everything, except I stopped short of telling her I was lonely. I didn't tell her how much I wanted her to be my wife.

I sighed and kicked Bear into a trot.

I promised to be patient. I didn't want Lilian to feel pressured if she wasn't ready to marry me.

But I never asked. Not even casually. I mean, I could ask her without the formal proposal. That was the honest thing to do.

Once I arrived home, I took my saddle off Bear. Then I took my sweet time brushing him out.

"What do you think?" I asked him.

I waited. He nudged my arm.

"You think I should ask her?"

His head bobbed up and down.

I rolled my eyes. Bear could not know what I was talking about.

I rubbed my hand on his face. "Good night, Bear."

He snorted.

I smiled as I walked back to my empty house. Bear sure was more vocal than Sergeant. I supposed he was growing on me.

When I entered the house, I lit a lamp. Then I sat in a chair and faced the cold fireplace. Late August was still fairly warm, too warm to build a fire.

Lord, show me what to do. Should I ask Lilian? Should I

wait?

Silence settled over the room.

Maybe I should buy the ring. Have it for when I worked up the courage to ask.

CHAPTER 34

September 9, 1893

JUSTINE

My wedding morning dawned with a cool breeze. I sipped a coffee while I sat on the back porch. By the time the day was over, I would be Mrs. Grady Thatcher.

I smiled.

Thank you, Lord, for bringing Grady into my life.

Years of tears. Years of prayers. Years hoping for God to rescue me from my horrible childhood home. Years of asking for a godly man. Years believing that one day God would answer me.

Today was that day. I would start my new life with my husband. We would face whatever life threw our way with kindness and grace. No raised fists. No fear for my safety.

I sipped my coffee and watched as the pinks and oranges of dawn faded to silver and blue. Then the sun rose and warmed my face, then my chest, then my entire being.

Any nervousness I had melted away in the quiet morning. More important than the love we shared was the faith we shared. Our faith in God would sustain us in the years to come.

I was not naïve. I knew life would bring us heartache and happiness, joys and sorrows, fears and peace. None of it mattered. We would face it together.

I prayed God would show us how to lift each other up. That He would guide us on our journey together.

"Morning," a voice came from the other side of the fence.

I smiled. "Grady? You know it's bad luck to see the bride before the wedding."

"Ha, you and I don't believe in luck."

I chuckled. "No, we don't."

He pulled himself up to peer over the fence. "I hope you're not wearing that."

"Well, you'll just have to wait and see, won't you?"

"Open the gate."

I stood and walked over to the fence. "I don't think so."

"Fine. You don't know what you're missing."

"I'm not missing a thing. Tonight I'll be your wife. What could possibly compare to that?"

"Come here."

I stood on my tiptoes.

"I love you, Justine Harper, almost Thatcher."

I giggled. "I love you, Grady Thatcher."

He reached his hand over the fence. I took it and squeezed.

"That was it. Just wanted to tell you first thing this morning."

"Alright."

"And every morning."

"See you at the church," I said.

"Bye, my sweet Justine."

I went back to my chair and coffee. I saw him between

the slats of the fence. Then he raised his arm above the fence line and waved before he disappeared.

Hours later, my family took me to the church. Lilian and Hayley helped me into the white gown. Grady told me to have a dress made just for our wedding. He covered the cost and told me to get exactly what a princess might want.

I kept it frugal, yet elegant.

When it slid down over my shoulders, Hayley jumped up and down and clapped. I was so glad we got her to Prescott before she lost her joy for life.

"You look gorgeous!" She hugged me, then released me quickly. "Oh, I don't want to wrinkle it."

Lilian pinned my hair back on the sides. When she finished, she kissed my cheek.

"I'm so proud of you, Justine. And I'm so happy for you."

"Your day will come soon enough," I whispered.

"Ah, but today is your day. Shall we let the boys in?"

The second Shane caught sight of me, his eyes reddened. He said nothing. I knew he was thinking about the years of sacrifice and pain. I knew what my wedding represented for the six of us. A new life far better than we dreamed possible.

He kissed my cheek and offered me his arm. Ike took my other arm. Flynn would have to wait, as both he and Deacon stood with Grady.

My brothers led me to the foyer. As Hayley walked up the aisle, I imagined a day in a few years when it would be her turn. Then Lilian walked up the aisle. I glanced at Deacon and saw him blink back tears. He clearly longed for his own wedding day with Lilian.

With Shane on one side and Ike on the other, I walked toward Grady. He grinned from ear to ear. Then he winked at me. I smiled. I teased him for days, saying I was pretty sure he was gonna cry during our wedding. He told me there wasn't a chance of that happening.

When the pastor asked who gave me away, all five of my siblings gathered around me, something totally unscripted. Then they shouted, "We do!"

I laughed as I faced Grady.

Then his eyes misted just a little. So did mine. I promised to love him, to obey, to have, to hold. I promised whether we faced sickness or health, joys or sorrows, whatever came, I would be his. Then he promised the same to me. We exchanged rings.

Then the pastor told him he could kiss me. He wiggled his eyebrows and kissed me senseless as the pastor announced us as Mr. and Mrs. Grady Thatcher.

Before I knew it, he leaned down and lifted me into his arms.

"What are you doing?"

"Running away with my princess."

I laughed as he carried me to the back of the church. Then he set my feet on the ground, turned toward the watching guests, and took a bow.

Then we went outside for our reception. My heart filled nearly to bursting.

GRADY

My wife. Justine was my wife. I smiled at her as we sat at the front table. Then I leaned forward and kissed her softly.

She smiled at me.

I looked at the crowd of friends and family. Will and

Hannah Colter told me my parents would be so proud of me. Ellie Mae echoed the sentiment the night before. Sam and Ellie Mae talked excitedly as Violet held Ashley. Boone and Jaclyn held hands until they sat down. Deacon sat next to me. Flynn, Ike, and Shane sat on his other side, while Lilian and Hayley sat on the other side of Justine.

James didn't make it. I learned he left for Chicago to see the World's Fair with his sweetheart before he received the invitation. Preston missed it, too. He took a job up near Ash Fork and couldn't make it back. I hoped he would for Deacon's wedding whenever that happened.

I was not born a Colter, but they adopted me into their family, and now the Harpers were, too.

I leaned over and whispered to Deacon, "When are you going to ask Lilian?"

He cleared his throat. "I bought the ring yesterday."

My eyes widened. "You did?"

He nodded, but refused to spill any more details. That was fine. He didn't need my help as much as I first thought. He picked out the perfect birthday gift all those months ago. I'm certain the ring was too expensive and perfect.

As the afternoon faded to evening, I stood and took Justine in my arms. "Let's go home."

She smiled and laced her fingers with mine. Then we walked the few blocks to our four-bedroom home.

After I carried her across the threshold, I set her down.

"Just so you know," I said. "I plan on filling every one of those bedrooms."

"Just once or twice each?"

I laughed. "I guess we'll have to wait and see."

Then I led her up to our room and thoroughly enjoyed our wedding night.

CHAPTER 35

LILIAN

Justine's wedding was beautiful. She was beautiful. Their love was beautiful.

I dabbed at my eyes as they left. I prayed they would experience more happiness than sadness. More joy than sorrow. I wanted the best for them.

"Lil?"

I smiled as Deacon sat in Hayley's chair next to me.

"It was lovely," I said without looking at him. The words came out sounding sadder than I intended.

"It was."

He took my hand in his. "Lil?"

I turned to face him.

"Do you think you're ready for a wedding of our own?"

I hesitated. I didn't think he was officially asking. "When you are ready to ask me, I have an answer for you and I think you will like it."

I smiled as he leaned closer and kissed my cheek.

"Would you be willing to move to the ranch when we marry?"

I sighed. "I don't know. Ike is in school. I'm working.

It's kinda far from town."

"You won't have to work if you don't want to. I earn plenty to provide for us and our family, whether that family is your siblings living with us or children of our own."

We never discussed it. I just assumed I would keep working.

"Ike will be in school for a few more years. I'm not sure I want him going that far alone."

Deacon smiled. "He wouldn't be. He could ride in with me when I go to work. Then, after school, he can work for Thomas until it's time for us to ride home together."

I drummed my fingers on the table. "I suppose that would work."

"Before you say something about us being newlyweds and needing privacy, we would have it. Our room is on the first floor. He would be on the second."

I smiled at him. "Clearly you've thought this through."

He shrugged. "I've had a lot of time alone lately."

I yawned, and he stood.

"Let me walk you home."

"Alright, let me just talk to Shane."

I walked over to Shane and told him I was leaving. Hayley walked with us, so Shane was going to bring Ike when he was ready to leave.

Then Hayley walked ahead of us. She bounded into the house when we arrived.

I lingered on the porch with Deacon.

"Will you come out for supper after church tomorrow? Bring Hayley, Shane, and Ike."

"Alright." I yawned again.

He smiled and pulled me into his arms. "Just a quick kiss, and then I'll let you go."

He lowered his head and brushed his lips across mine.

Then he released his hold.

"Good night, Lil."

"Good night."

As I readied for bed, I hoped Deacon would ask me soon and that all his talk of our future was real.

The next day after church, we headed out to Colter Ranch. When we crested the hill overlooking the ranch, I smiled as I remembered the first time I rode out there, concerned for Grady's life. I was too afraid then to appreciate the beauty of the ranch. Now I soaked it in like the dry ground after a monsoon rain.

I could live at the ranch surrounded by Deacon's family. They were the kindest, most welcoming people I knew. From the first time I met his parents, I knew they were the complete opposite of mine and exactly the type of people I wished were my parents.

When Shane pulled the wagon to a stop, Deacon helped me down. Then he laced his fingers with mine.

Instead of walking toward the house, he led me along the path to his house.

"I've never shown you my house. It's time for you to see it."

When he opened the door, I smiled. The chairs at the table were evenly spaced. It reminded me of the day we met and he fixed the brand wall. He showed me the parlor, the washroom with indoor plumbing, and his room.

"That would be ours."

My heart thrummed at the look in his eyes. I let go of his hand and headed upstairs. He stayed downstairs.

"There are two rooms up there," he hollered. "One is kinda big, so we could split it into two rooms if we need to."

I looked around. Ike could take the bigger room. He

would be on his own long before we would need that room.

"I like it," I said as I joined him downstairs.

He took my hand again. Then he led me around the side of the house to the porch which faced the lake. Two chairs and a small table gave the perfect vantage point for watching sunsets.

"It's breathtaking."

"Not as breathtaking as you." His voice sounded husky.

My pulse raced. Then he dropped to one knee. Oh, my!

He reached into his pocket and pulled out a ring.

"Lil, I love you. I love your big heart. Thank you for overlooking my odd behavior. I love your smile. I love your blue eyes and that cute freckle near your left one."

He winked at me, and I smiled.

"I've told you before, but I'll say it again. I want you to be my wife and to spend the rest of my days with you by my side. Will you marry me?"

I dropped to my knees in front of him, which totally caught him by surprise.

"Deacon, I want to be your wife. I want to be your equal. I want us to raise my brother and our children in a home full of love and respect."

"That was a 'yes'?"

"Yes."

He slid the ring onto my finger. Then he stood and helped me to my feet.

I wrapped my arms around him and parted my lips as he lowered his to mine. He kissed me deeply, urgently, which pulled my heart closer to his as I returned his kiss.

"Lilian!" Hayley's voice sounded from the front of the house. "Oh, there you are."

Deacon ignored her and slowed the kiss when he wanted to, despite the audience. I released my arms from him and smiled the entire way to the big house.

CHAPTER 36

December 25, 1893

DEACON

Lilian wanted to marry on Christmas Day, so we waited three incredibly long months to get married. It was good. It gave us a chance to let my brothers know so they could all come home. Even Preston came, having arrived the night before.

No one lived in George and Maggie Larson's house since they moved out earlier in the year after George had a stroke. It was nice seeing how much better he looked at Thanksgiving. Maggie was the one that suggested we could use it for guests or family reunions.

So, we moved all the furniture out of the parlor. We took down the wall to one bedroom, which added more space to the parlor. Then we lined the room with tables and chairs. Lilian and Hayley stayed in two of the remaining bedrooms on Christmas Eve. They spent the day decorating for our wedding. I had yet to see it, but everyone told me how spectacular it looked.

"You almost ready?" Papa asked as he stood in the doorway of my room.

"I can't figure out this tie."

Papa laughed. "I know how you feel. Let me get James."

I stopped messing with the blasted thing. I pulled at the collar of my shirt. A suit. I was wearing a suit.

"James!" Papa yelled out the door.

A few minutes later, James entered. He squinted.

"Deacon, is that you?" he teased. "I barely recognize you without your denim pants and cowboy hat."

"Just help me with this tie."

He laughed. In two seconds, with some magic hand movements, he righted the thing.

"There you go."

"Is Grady here?" I asked. "And Preston?"

"They are over at the lodge. That's what our wives are calling it."

"Come on, son. Don't want to be late for your own wedding."

I followed Papa across the yard to the newly dubbed lodge. Grady and Preston greeted me. I hugged Preston extra-long, so glad to see he was still sober after roughly nine months. Maybe he finally dealt with his demons. I was glad to have him stand with me.

Grady was the one that suggested Preston be my best man instead of him. I was torn about it until he told me he thought it would mean a lot to Preston.

They decorated the room with boughs of pine, pine-cones, red ribbons, and other touches that made the place feel like we were outdoors on a snowy winter day. The fireplaces blazed with a welcoming glow. The Harpers and Colters made the room feel peaceful and homey. I felt honored that my wedding was the first Colter celebration at the lodge.

I stood at the front with Preston to my left and Grady to his. I shifted my weight from foot to foot as I waited for my bride.

"Here she comes!" Ellie Mae said. "Take your places."

Hayley stood across the aisle, with Justine beside her.

Then the doors opened, and my Lil entered the room. My heart froze as I studied her. Her long strawberry blond hair cascaded down her back to her waist. I hadn't realized it was so long.

The dress looked stunning on her, and it showed off her beauty. I did not know she was having a dress made for the day. I supposed I should have expected it when she suggested I wear a suit.

My eyes snagged on her earlobes. The pearl dangling earrings. She wore them. My heart filled with joy.

When my gaze connected with hers, I started breathing again. She grinned as she walked up the aisle alone, which she said represented the Harper family's break from their past.

When she stopped and turned toward me, I could barely believe the time had finally arrived. We said our vows. We exchanged the rings. Then it was over. She was mine, and I was hers.

"You may kiss your bride."

I pulled her close and kissed her like I never had before, perhaps a little more passionately than I should have in front of such a large audience. Boone hooted when I finally released my wife.

Lilian's cheeks turned red and her eyes sparkled. "That was some kiss."

"Just wanted to make sure you know I love you."

She laughed. "No doubt whatsoever."

After an hour of celebrating with our families, I escorted

her to our home, and I led her to our bedroom.

"How are you feeling about tonight?" I asked, as I suspected she might be nervous or fearful after what Caleb had done to her.

"Nervous."

I held her hands. "I promise you, I won't hurt you, and I won't ask you for anything that you don't want to give."

She let out a shaky breath. "Maybe if you kiss me like you did earlier."

She laughed nervously.

I gently pulled her into my arms. Then I kissed her slowly, building to something more passionate. I paid close attention to her response.

"Deacon?" Her breaths came in quick puffs. "I'm as ready as I'll ever be."

I took that exactly as she meant it and made her my wife.

EPILOGUE

Colter Ranch
December 25, 1897

LILIAN

"Do you have Stella?" I asked. "We're going to be late."

"Don't worry. They won't start supper without us," Deacon said as he set our toddler on his shoulders.

"Horsey!" Stella squealed as she grabbed two handfuls of his hair.

"Not so tight, baby girl."

"Papa go!"

He grabbed my hand and pulled me toward the door. "You heard her. Let's go."

I laughed as we hurried across the yard to the lodge. I opened the door to a whirlwind of noise.

Over the past four years, Deacon and his brothers worked on the building to reinforce the roof and make the space wide open. Good thing too, as our family only grew larger and larger year after year.

I rubbed my back, and Justine noticed.

"Are you pregnant?"

"Justine!"

"Well, are you?"

"I think so. Maybe three months."

"Does Deacon know?"

"He's the one that figured it out first."

Justine laughed as she shifted her almost two-year-old Justin to her other hip. Little Lee tugged on her skirt. She placed a hand on his head.

"Time for presents?" he asked.

"Not yet. Go see if you can find Papa."

Lee hurried away.

Shane came over and greeted us. Still single. My heart ached for him. He turned thirty-one that year and seemed no closer to settling down. Perhaps it was because he spent so much of his early adult life caring for us.

Hayley bounded over and hugged all of us Harpers. She was still single too, but at twenty-two, I didn't worry about her. She would find the right man soon.

Flynn joined us.

"I heard you were courting a lovely young lady," I teased him.

"Maybe."

I scanned the room. None of us were sure if Ike would be there. In the last letter I had from him, he couldn't decide if he was going to come visit on his break at university or if he was going to work.

As the meal started, I sighed. I hoped he would make it.

"He'll be here," Deacon said. "He wired yesterday and said he was taking the train up."

"You didn't tell me."

"Sorry. I was a little distracted last night celebrating our anniversary early."

Heat warmed my cheeks. "Distracted. Is that what you call it?"

He grinned as I shook my head.

Will called us all to settle down. Then he offered an eloquent prayer. Instead of bowing my head like I should, I cataloged all those in attendance.

Will and Hannah, as always, sat at the head of the table. Ellie Mae, Sam, their five children. Boone, Jaclyn, and their two children. James, Keri, and their son and daughter. Grady, Justine with their two sons, Lee and Justin. Me, Deacon, and Stella. Preston, his wife, and their sons. Violet was alone after being left at the altar. My heart still hurt for her.

Then there was Keri's family, the Glassmans. The Andersons for three generations. Adam and Julia Larson and their children and grandchildren.

"Amen." Deacon parroted back.

"We might need to expand the lodge soon," I said.

"We are truly blessed this year that everyone is home," he said right as the door swung open.

A burst of cold air whooshed into the room with Ike. I smiled as he shook off the snow from his boots.

"Did you know we are getting a white Christmas?" he said as he came over and kissed my cheek.

"Maybe you'll stay for a few days then."

"A week. I have to be back for work before school starts again."

He sat in the empty chair next to Hayley.

As the conversation buzzed and food passed around the table, my heart filled to overflowing. In my wildest dreams, I never pictured being a part of such a wonderful family.

When I married my resourceful stockman four years ago, I thought I couldn't be any happier. Looking around the room, I wondered if my happiness would ever stop increasing.

"What are you thinking about?" Deacon asked.

"I'm proud to be part of the Colter family."

"Aren't you glad I rearranged your brand wall?"

I laughed. "I suppose you think that was when I fell in love with you."

"Wasn't it?"

"No. I think it was when you stood up to Xavier for calling me Valentine."

He laughed. "I completely forgot about that."

"And you fell in love with me the moment you laid eyes on me," I said with confidence.

"Of course. I'm not blind, you know. I knew you were the prettiest woman I would ever meet."

Then he leaned over and kissed me.

"Happy anniversary, Lil."

My heart filled with a deeper joy than I thought possible. I found my godly man and the family I always wanted.

AUTHOR'S NOTE

When I initially mapped out the Colter Sons Series, there was no Grady Thatcher. I intended book 4 to be Deacon's story alone. Yet, once I introduced Grady's character in book 1 and proclaimed him as an instant friend to Deacon, I knew there was no possible way to tell Deacon's story without telling Grady's.

In the end, I was very pleased with the way their friendship provided such rich material. In some ways, I imagined their friendship much like that of David and Jonathan in 1 Samuel. In other ways, their friendship was reminiscent of the bond between men who fight in battle together.

How did I arrive at the idea of livestock inspectors? It was a bizarre journey to get there. I originally wanted to make them Arizona Rangers, but my timeline was about eight years before the Rangers were formed, and I hate claiming "creative liberty" in situations like that.

Then I came across a snippet in a book about the territorial legislatures of Arizona from the 1860's to 1912. In 1887, the Stock and Sanitary Law was passed and ratified by Governor Zulick. This was the catalyst for forming the Livestock Sanitary Commission which included the appointment of a Veterinary Surgeon General. On March 19, 1891, the first livestock inspectors were appointed for each county in Arizona. Those real dates fit perfectly into my timeline. Also, the responsibilities of the original livestock inspectors were twofold: monitor for disease and enforce brand registration. This also fit with Grady and Deacon's veterinary back-grounds.

During my research, I came across *Calling the Brands* by Monte McCord. This was a great resource that helped me understand branding rules, how to read a brand, and why livestock inspectors were a critical component to civilizing the West. That book also detailed how livestock inspectors alone could not curtail rustling. Despite all their hard work, very few rustlers were ever prosecuted. Like you, I would not have been happy with anything less than the capture and prosecution of the rustlers that killed Grady's parents, so that's what I wrote, even though it would have been very unlikely to happen in real life.

Because I built up Deacon and Grady's friendship throughout the series, I really thought it would be fun if they fell in love with sisters so they would at least become brothers-in-law.

Though much of the Harper's childhood is heartbreaking, it was more common in the Wild West than one might expect. Deadbeat parents, abusive parents, and molesters have walked the earth for millennia. Good, kind-hearted people deal with the fallout of this in their own lives. I write about these things because I want to encourage those who have been victims of such atrocities that there is hope for a new life, a different life, full of healing.

Deacon's odd behavior is a form of obsessive-compulsive disorder. My husband and I often ask the question: How did people back then cope with _____? Mental illness, cancer, disorders, and the like. I wanted to explore how a godly man might cope with his weaknesses which he felt helpless to control. Though it was a source of pain in his life, it also came with some gifts, which he did acknowledge.

Anyway, it was my pleasure to share Deacon and Lilian's story along with the bonus story of Grady and Justine. The saga continues with Preston's story in: *The Restless Wrangler (Colter Sons Book 5)*.

Karen Baney

———

Want More Arizona Territory Romance?

Get a FREE novella featuring characters connected to the Colter Sons series! Plus exclusive updates on new releases, special offers, and historical insights from the frontier.

Subscribe at: books.karenbaney.com/larson–christmas

ABOUT THE AUTHOR

Karen Baney is passionate about writing stories full of flawed characters. She enjoys weaving together stories of second chances, redemption, and overcoming personal trials. As a transplant to Arizona, she loves researching the state's history and finding ways to seamlessly incorporate real history and real settings into her novels. In addition to writing and speaking, Karen works as a Software Development Manager for a Christian ministry.

Her faith plays an important role both in her life and in her writing. Karen and her husband, Jim, make their home in Gilbert, Arizona, with their two dogs, Bella and Daisy. Both Jim and Karen are active at Rock Point Church in Queen Creek, Arizona.

Discover faith-laced stories with characters who feel like lifelong friends.

Visit www.karenbaney.com to discover more historical romance series set in the American West. Follow Karen's writing journey and get behind-the-scenes glimpses of her research adventures on social media.

Facebook:	@AuthorKarenBaney
X:	@karen_baney
Instagram:	@AuthorKarenBaney
BookBub:	Follow Karen Baney for new release alerts

BOOKS BY KAREN BANEY

Historical Western Romance
Prescott Pioneers Series:
Step back in time to the wild, untamed Arizona Territory where survival depends on grit, faith, and the courage to start over. Follow three pioneer families—the Andersons, Colters, and Larsons—as they risk everything for the promise of a new life in a land that demands both strength and hope.

A Dream Unfolding
A Heart Renewed
A Life Restored
A Hope Revealed
Hidden Prospects

Desert Manna Series:
Sometimes the most beautiful love stories bloom in the desert. Set in the growing frontier town of Prescott during the early 1870s, these tender romances follow women rebuilding their lives after heartbreak and the unexpected men who help them discover that second chances at love are worth the risk. Set in Prescott, Arizona between 1871 - 1873.

Beauty for Ashes
Joy for Mourning
Oaks of Justice

Colter Sons Series:
Power, legacy, and forbidden love collide in this sweeping family saga set in the Arizona Territory. The Colter ranch

empire has weathered decades of frontier life, but now family secrets and buried betrayals threaten to destroy everything. As five brothers—and one resilient sister—navigate the treacherous waters of love, loss, and redemption, they must decide what's worth fighting for. Set in Prescott and other locations within the Arizona Territory in 1887 - 1906.

The Reluctant Cattleman
The Roaming Adventurer
The Railroad Magnate
The Resourceful Stockman
The Restless Wrangler
The Resilient Bride

Larson Sisters Series

Meet the next generation! These delightful novellas follow the three daughters of Adam and Julia Larson from the *Prescott Pioneers Series* as they navigate love, courtship, and finding their own happily ever afters in territorial Arizona in 1886 – 1894.

In Love at Christmas
In Love with the Rancher
In Love with the Horse Trainer

Contemporary Romance

Vargas Ranch Series:

Love is in the air at the Vargas Guest Ranch & Resort near Wickenburg, Arizona. Meet the Vargas family—five swoon-worthy brothers and their cousins who live by their family motto: "We do not deviate from the Lord's plan."

These rugged cowboys run a successful working ranch and luxury resort while navigating the rollercoaster of finding true love.

Falling for a Fake Cowboy
Falling for a Real Cowboy
Honeymoon with a Real Cowboy
Falling for a Shy Cowboy
Falling for a Bossy Cowboy
Falling for a Smart Cowboy
Falling for a Humbug Cowboy
Falling for a Devoted Cowgirl
Falling for a Pregnant Cowgirl
Falling for a Cowboy's Legacy

Steadfast Love Series:

The *Steadfast Love* series follows a close-knit group of friends as they navigate the beautiful mess of modern life in the Phoenix area—workplace drama, complicated families, and love that shows up when they least expect it. These contemporary romances blend emotional depth with authentic faith, reminding us that even when life unravels, God's love never does.

The Heart I Rescue (prequel)
The Air I Breathe

I'd wasted my life and had given up on second chances.

I should have died that night...

It should have been me instead of him.

My name is Preston Colter. After spending years destroying my life and every relationship, I'm finally done with drinking and drifting. I'm not sure I can overcome the demons of my past, even with God on my side.

No one will hire me because of my past. A single mother is the only one willing to take a chance on my sorry hide—despite our history. It has me wondering if her son...

Naw. Couldn't be mine, right?

———

If you love emotionally rich Christian romance with rugged frontier grit…

Janette Oke meets Louis L'Amour. Mary Connealy meets Zane Grey.

The *Colter Sons* series blends heartfelt faith journeys, masculine coming-of-age arcs, and sweeping Arizona history into unforgettable love stories.

DESERT LIFE MEDIA

———

Desert Life Media: *There Is Life in The Desert*

Entertainment–first Christian fiction set in the Southwest, featuring redemption, family, and faith

Publishing clean, wholesome, and uplifting fiction since 2010

———

desertlifemedia.com

www.ingramcontent.com/pod-product-compliance
Lightning Source LLC
Chambersburg PA
CBHW061947170626
46813CB00006B/2565